CN00821361

UNREDACTED EXPLETIVES

A collection of short stories

Christopher C James

Silver Quill Publishing

ISBN: 978-1-80440-230-6
Silver Quill Publishing
www.silverquillpublishing.com

The Pink Gin Chronicles

'They're with a publisher, you know?'
The bloated man slumped against the bar near the Air Ambulance collection box, a puny vinyl stool lost in the immensity of his arse, appears to have awoken with a start and bellows the words across the sleepy sparseness of an early afternoon session in the Black Lion.

Eyebrows barely flicker. Nobody has asked, and nobody is interested. He's been banging on the same shit to anyone who'll listen for some years and these days, they're all hardened non-listeners. There is a confused but amused silence amongst the smattering of dog-eared human remnants parading themselves in the half-light of a late, liquid lunch.

He is referring to his cherished life's work, the poems and short stories which he believes, with admirable conviction, immediately sets him a few steps higher up the evolutionary ladder than these lesser mortals.

He is, of course, in dispute with said publisher and if pressed, can't find a good word to say on the matter. The faceless entity with a pompous name, elaborate letterhead and forwarding address of a post office box off the Old Compton Road, had indeed pulled a royal fast one on him, securing from him a sizeable up-front fee before paying scant regard to any contractual obligations on their part. His precious collected scribblings have subsequently been locked in a literary purgatory awaiting the promised next phase of publication which, five years down the line, has yet to materialise.

Maurice Harris-Williams is something of a fixture in

the Black Lion, as much a part of the place as the Guinness tap from which he derives his daily inspiration. He is well-known, and not much liked. He is a self-proclaimed cunt, which leaves little latitude for others to express their personal levels of loathing.

He is probably younger than most would guess but he is negligent to minor trifles such as appearance and personal hygiene. The remnants of thinning hair hang limply at shoulder length and his chins are multiple. The Guinness has taken its toll on his middle-aged midriff which flops unattractively over the beltline of bulging denim jeans. Those unassuming souls entering from the side door of the Black Lion may feel unsettled by a fine, unrestricted view of the crack of his arse as he leans forward against the bar caressing his pint. Although unfairly compared in size to the Vale of Glamorgan itself, some are of the opinion that this is his best feature, and one glimpse should be sufficient deterrent against entering into any sort of discourse with him.

He is, of course, unmarried and as far as anyone is aware, has no overtly romantic aspirations whatsoever. Although just occasionally, a whimsical expression of lonely longing can be observed passing like a shadow across his ruddy features as Dierdre, with her voluptuous, feminine curves draws him another pint of the black stuff and presents it to him with something approaching a warm bonhomie.

No one is sure where his money has come from, certainly not from the rewards of any of his literary offerings, but he's tight with it and orders for himself another top-up without invitation to the usual collection of sots, propping up the bar in various withering states of sobriety. Sometimes on a good day, he would follow up the Guinness with a Drambuie chaser. On less good days, the Drambuie on repeat serves sufficiently as his sole solace.

The scar that catches attention in the centre of his forehead is a consequence of an excised skin cancer, he asserts, but many suspect that it was the work of a hammer in his earlier life. Knowing him makes this theory all the more plausible. Traumatic damage to his frontal lobes may yet be the kindest explanation for his behaviour.

He is not unaware that they all think of him as something of an arse and rather revels in his unpopularity. When he goes outside for one of his frequent cigarette breaks, he is largely ignored by passers-by, despite having resided in the town for most of his life. He prefers it this way.

He owns an aging, mossy-windowed Volvo estate on the roof of which he used to transport unfeasibly large hulks of furniture to and from his antique shop. These days the shop is closed more than it's open, and even if his boasted privileged relationship with a wealthy importer from Chicago were true, it would still be insufficient to cover his extravagant monthly bar expenditure.

So, as the cloying pungency of conjecture wafts through the air, the town tongues enjoy a good wag.

The bastard son of the Seventh Earl of Glanavon has been a lingering favourite untruth for years. His superior ways, the double-barrel surname and his use of words that no one else understands, hint of higher breeding. But the devil is in the detail, and elder folk in town can still remember his mother as a prim, uptight, English church-type who wouldn't even allow herself usage of the word 'damn', let alone open her legs for an over-exuberant member of the landed gentry.

The town boys of a certain age all have their own story about what he had tried to entice them to do for a fiver in the rhododendrons in the park; outright lies sculpted haphazardly into a new truth to which many have subsequently subscribed. Thus, arose another theory that he is in fact the ringleader of an international paedophile network, involved in people trafficking via some of the more discreet coastal coves out west, keeping his victims locked up for days at a time in the labyrinth of dusty Victorian oak wardrobes at the back of his shop.

Lending gravitas to this otherwise extravagantly oblique rumour is the almost perpetual presence of Lucas Van De Pohl at his side, sullenly sipping pink gins. Alienated in the town for his choice of beverage, his Dutch accent, and most of all for his candid homosexuality, he has become an unlikely drinking partner. Apart from sharing the same view of the barmaid's bulging cleavage and the odd unsavoury political view, they have few mutual interests, and there is little love lost between the two.

Lucas drops effortlessly back into his native tongue the more he drinks. In extremes of inebriation, he expresses some amusingly guttural phrases, especially relating to Maurice and his inflated aspirations as an author. But most of the time, like the great scribe himself, he is content to spend his thirsty hours giving the thousand-yard stare to the inverted spirit bottles, fidgeting with beermats. Much time has evaporated with the two sitting in laconic contemplation, occasionally extemporising the odd, poorly considered opinion about what is wrong with the world today. Misunderstood would be the kindest way of putting it; the pair are viewed in measured, contemptuous suspicion by their fellow drinkers.

In the same way that Maurice's origins are blurry, collective memory did not extend far back enough to recall how such an outright misfit as Lucas had blown into this obscure corner of the globe and effortlessly installed himself almost immediately as an obvious subject of disdain. Unknown to him, he bore striking physical resemblances to a leading character in one of Maurice's racier tales, who had been a fugitive diamond smuggler from Antwerp, fond of absinthe, and tortured mercilessly by Russian mercenaries before meeting a remarkably gory demise on the end of a Kalashnikov bayonet.

Living in a place well-acquainted with prejudiced opinions and brutal ways, and given the collected views held by many of the townsfolk and all of the pub regulars, it was surprising that Maurice and Lucas hadn't received more in the way of physical threat over the years. The deterrent is as simple as it is loyal, and the dog is every bit as reprehensible as the owner.

Mingus, of mixed parentage but without question possessing a generous dollop of ugly English Bull Terrier DNA, was responsible for several illegitimate litters around the environs. Unless baited, he customarily sits quietly, at the foot of Maurice's barstool, licking his testicles and breaking wind with vicious effect. Looking mean, like a canine version of a skinhead, his standard demeanour doesn't encourage friendly petting. Those too drunk to be insensitive to his general malevolence will be reminded by a brooding low-pitched growl and a baring of yellow teeth if they approach too close.

Maurice likes it when people ask about the dog's name because it gives him the opportunity to be effortlessly pretentious in his knowledge of jazz music, a superfluous talent in the closed-minded, backwaters of Mid-Wales.

Another sup, and daggers are exchanged across the bar with Teddy's florid features, reclined as usual in his powered wheelchair by the fruit machine, wearing most of the contents of a bag of cheese and onion crisps down his front. There's history there. The mysterious series of events that saw two simultaneous flat tyres during one of Teddy's protracted post-Mackeson snoozes, followed only days later by Mingus suffering a prolonged and memorable bout of diarrhoea, thought to be caused by the accidental ingestion of chocolate.

As no one local had read, nor was ever likely to read his work, his short stories allow Maurice a valuable vehicle for retribution. They are a sweet catharsis for decades of pent-up bile, and rejection.

Teddy, for example, had met several drawn out and bloody ends within the pages of Maurice's secret world. A striking number of his villains found themselves the victims of some or other misfortune and languished miserably in powered wheelchairs. A recent addition to the collection was about a tyrannical Albanian criminal mastermind, whose wheeled escape from the CIA had been foiled by getting stuck on a railway crossing, with inevitable consequences.

Of Maurice's collected works, a personal favourite features Deirdre, the generously proportioned puller-of-pints, colloquially known for reasons unworthy of explanation, as The Dartboard. It describes, in fairly direct purple prose, how she became the property of a wealthy Arab oil mogul in her earlier life by virtue of a losing poker hand, before subsidising her burgeoning crystal meth habit as a prostitute on the streets of Athens. Riven with venereal disease, she had been rescued by a Trappist Order of Nasturtium Monks who, tainted by rumours of connections to the Mafia, settled in inconspicuous obscurity in a retreat just outside Wrexham. There, she met her current partner, Dilwyn, working as a magician's assistant with the scars to prove it, and who is in fact, a eunuch. But that particular thread of the story will be tantalisingly saved for the prequel.

Having spent days surveying the gnarled, tattooed knuckles of Brian James whose customary seating arrangement orientates him directly to the right of Maurice, it had been a simple matter to concoct a back history far more entertaining than the truth. He had broken jaws for a pastime in the nineteen sixties London gang wars, the same pair of hands throttling throats of grasses and digging shallow graves in the Essex marshes. Bad gout and repeated nightly visitations from corpses with gaping necks, in various states of decomposition had eventually forced an early retirement to the safe anonymity of a Welsh rural community. They may yet catch up with him.

Venturing into the unchartered, and somewhat uncomfortable, territory of science fiction, a characteristically rambling tale chronicles the journey of Alvin Owen, an alien from the distant galaxy of Zorg Minor, audaciously planted in Wales as a spy many generations ago when the slate mines above the town were still working. Switching allegiances over the years from Napoleon's Army to the Prussian Empire to the Irish Republican Movement, he escaped death on numerous occasions through his ability to regenerate severed parts of his anatomy. The Russians are the current beneficiaries from his work as a postman, compiling regular reports on the town's activities, local interpretations of BBC news reports and information on individuals of interest, this being the main reason for lengthy hours he spends in silence in the Black Lion. His cigarette lighter continues to record conversations of interest.

Beneath his benign, bespectacled, exterior, Wallace Nicholls is burdened by many terrible secrets. From humble beginnings as a street pickpocket in Paris, via a circuitous route, involving a Hungarian drug smuggler, a horse trader from Alabama and a Geisha girl with a passing acquaintance to President Kennedy, he had travelled the world as a kitchen porter on a merchant vessel before discovering a vision of God in the bottom of a vodka glass, thus committing the rest of his life to the worship thereof.

Maurice shakes his head in smug contemplation, bathing indulgently in his yet-to-be-discovered literary brilliance. He'll sue those pompous arses in London and take his precious manuscript to someone more worthy. Then they'll be sorry.

Mingus is restive. Roused from his self-congratulatory stupor by the dog's pacing and panting, Maurice notices that Lucas's drink hasn't been touched for a while. The ice has melted and the cherry, which he always insists upon, is starting to look bloated.

Keep up, Dutch.

He turns to his left, leaning backwards slightly and is surprised to find Lucas unconscious and propped limply against the wall. He frowns. The cheese-noshing bastard can normally tolerate industrial quantities of gin and they've only been installed in their usual spot just the three short hours since opening time.

Mingus is sniffing around under the stools and Maurice notices the puddle on the floor under Lucas's prostrate form. The daft Dutch fucker has pissed himself! He lets forth a throaty chortle and nudges him.

For fucks sake Dutch! What's going on? You putting Gordons on the cornflakes an again?

The nudge is enough to dislodge the smaller man from his stool and he sprawls flaccidly onto the tacky floor. Even the hefty thump fails to rouse him.

Deirdre leans over the bar, her cleavage bulging to unfeasible proportions.

Are you sure he's okay, Maurice? He's not normally this bad.

Maurice pokes Lucas with his toe, avoiding closer inspection of the expanding wet patch gathering on the seat of his trousers. There is no response.

He shrugs passively and assumes a composed aspect over the remainder of his Guinness while Deirdre phones 999. The rest of the bar gather in a confused, head-shaking circle around Lucas. Speaker phone on, Deirdre pushes through and kneels down beside him as she is instructed the basics of CPR by a calm Scottish accent. Her regulars observe her hypnotically undulating efforts in sozzled admiration.

Maurice is still placidly contemplating the situation from his vantage point at the bar when the paramedics tumble in, an efficient blur of perspiring bottle green. A double Drambuie, which he helped himself to in the absence of bar staff, has calmed his immediate discombobulation, and he is content to survey the resuscitation efforts with a glazed detachment from the safety of his barstool. Mingus is shooed away as he attempts to cock his leg on the defibrillator.

Maurice shakes his head in mute disbelief; it's been a quite remarkable interlude. A truly illuminating experience, and once again, The Black has not let him down in the provision of tasty subject matter. He glowers with a passing contempt at the emptiness of his glass and with a heft of breath, lifts himself falteringly from the unfortunate stool. Under the rubber mask, Lucas's face has turned a putrid puce colour leading Maurice to deduce that a less-than-optimal outcome is about to unfold. He yanks on the dog's lead and starts tiptoeing through the detritus of resuscitation towards the door.

Ah, the precious fragility of the human condition. Come, Minger. Serendipity has been kind. We have places to be and much to contemplate. Our brilliance must shineth elsewhere tonight. Adieu, mes amis.

No one registers his departure, a waft of dog fart in his wake; nor the absence of half a bottle of Drambuie from behind the bar.

Meanwhile in Gaza

She shuffles alone through the scrubby littoral carrying a gnawing hunger and a baking thirst. These familiar dunes, which had once been a place of play and pleasure. The pale sky is a crisscross of deathly vapour trails, each one signifying a new torment.

She continues to trudge south, searching in vain for a reason why this has all happened; what has she done wrong? Why had she been born to this arid hell? She has no twenty-four-hour TV channel to inform and debate the whys and wherefores. She will never meet, nor even know the names of these faceless men, with their fat bellies and inflated proclamations and denunciations, who will decide her fate. Safe in their towers of ivory, locking their egotistical horns over other people's lives.

She isn't even a pawn in their game, just a bystander, who only weeks before had led a normal life, going to school and playing with her friends in the impoverished, but safe streets. And now it's all just dust and blood. Animals skitter from ruin to ruin trying in vain to escape the cacophony of bombardment and the perpetual sound of jets. The stench of decay is everywhere.

She sees a nail on the floor. Half a finger still attached. There is a reverberating crack of gunfire in the distance. She bends down closer, to inspect her find and feels a zip of movement in the air where her head was. She doesn't know how unlucky she's been.

Dennis and Michael

I have become increasingly conscious of the uncomfortable predictability of my visits to his unprepossessing terraced house; the same time, the same day, the same trek up the uneven, potholed lane to the back gate, the same barked, vigilant greeting at the threshold of the open kitchen door, and the same supercilious voice booming out of the TV.

Only men of higher breeding can get away with the wearing of certain clothes, and Michael Portillo's green linen shirts and orange chinos jar with the grim circumstances in which I encounter his weekly documentaries on great train journeys. He is as far removed as it's possible to be from this wheezing pile of bones lying in front of me on the bed with cigarette burns on grey sheets. A bucket reposes on the threadbare, stained carpet under the bed, the surrounding wallpaper peels apologetically, and a cracked ceiling shares the same jaundiced hue as his skin.

This week, Michael's in Canada, trying to affect an interesting discourse with a dull, overweight man wearing over-sized spectacles, droning on about a cannon. Good gig if you can get it, I say. The quip is lost on Dennis, who is now deeply embedded in the depths of his slow dying process. Despite the frequency of my visits to this private purgatory, his permanent state of puzzlement leads me to question if he knows who I am.

He doesn't have much to show for the sixty-seven years his lungs have seen fit to support him, but now they've now called time and await their taxi to the Pearly Gates. With no prospect of recovery, he puffs on determinedly and undaunted.

We start by pretending that I don't notice the full ashtray, or the box of matches crudely concealed on the undershelf of his bedside table. Or the smell which hangs heavily in the sunbeams permeating through his torn, nicotine-tinged curtains. He lies there, avoiding eye contact, head bowed, like a contrite schoolboy awaiting his admonishment. Frustrating though it is from a professional angle, I realise that there's nothing gained by calling him out now. I've explained several times to him that his referral request for home oxygen, perhaps the one thing that could genuinely improve his current quality of life, has been declined because of the perceived fire risk, but he remains stubbornly resolute. He clings on to the tacit pride in his ability to construct the perfect rollie.

As a useful distraction during my visits, I always make a point of admiring the guitar on the stand in the corner next to the TV, perhaps reminding him of happier times when he still had the breath in him to sing out a song or two. The tuning pegs have gathered dust, and the strings are rusty, but the frets are worn, and it occupies pride of place, so I infer that it must have been an important presence in Dennis's previous life. It may be one of the few threads of achievement that a single man living in a small, impoverished, council terrace, smelling of stale tobacco, dog, and yesterday's microwave meal clung on to. I ponder asking him to bang out a tune for me, but I notice that his tremor has worsened, and he can barely muster enough strength to hold the cigarette which he's now feeling sufficiently comfortable to openly light up in front of me. I try to ignore the Swastikas he's self-tattooed on the backs of his hands; this is no time for political posturing, and they don't alter the fact that his days are now both dismal and numbered.

Sometimes, in an effort to find some neutral ground in the gaping abyss between us, and to delay straying onto other thornier issues, we talk about music. Over the course of my attendances, I have determined that perhaps unsurprisingly for his demographic, he is admirer of Seventies Heavy Rock. There are stacks of worn-looking CDs on a dusty shelf depicting demons, men in leather and scantily clad women with poodle haircuts blowing in the wind, waiting to grace the shelves of a high street charity shop. It's difficult to imagine him with a hirsute mane rather than the chemo-induced alopecia.

On the back step, Roly the corpulent mongrel is a ubiquitous presence and an attentive sentinel. As Dennis's illness has progressed and further diminished his previously slight frame, the dog has piled on the pounds through want of exercise. They're close though. Without his canine companionship, there is little doubt that Dennis would have already succumbed, and it's the constant worry about what will happen to Roly that keeps him breathing; and awake at night. His barking has spread unjustified fear amongst the less robust members of the district nursing team who visit twice daily believing him to be feral and dangerous. A warning has unnecessarily appeared on Dennis's medical records advising due care when approaching the fierce dog. It takes a fellow dog owner to recognise that it's all just hollow bravado and in reality, he's just as frightened and confused as his owner.

I search the room for threads on which to start a conversation and notice for the first time that the wallpaper with its patches of mould has a pattern of pink roses, a long-departed feminine touch in a house that could only be currently inhabited by an unwashed, scruffy man. Dennis is perched on his bed wearing his lost boy look and I decide that the decor could only be courtesy of his mother. God rest her soul.

He has a sister though. One that he never speaks to or of, after some half-forgotten family acrimony. A spindly, pinched woman who I recall meeting months before at the outset of his illness, when all parties were convened to decide how this should play out. In her subsequent absence, she has since clearly decided that she has no willingness to share precious moments of his final days. She has an undertaker and an estate agent lined up though, and the phone number for the RSPCA ready and waiting. I ask him about her and receive a cursory shake of the head, leaving me to wonder about what forbidden, bitter memories they share.

Roly is inside again, nuzzling at Dennis's hand and making an already fetid room marginally less pleasant. He is all dog breath-panting and licks, craving for attention in this shared misery. His loyalty is painfully touching and sharply contrasts with the Dennis's brittle human support network.

He is clearly not in the mood for conversation today but is unable to disguise his loneliness, and his wish for me to stay. He sets me about a task trying to find out how much Oramorph he still has stashed in the clutter of his kitchen. I skirt around Roly and trip on an aberrant strip of linoleum as I head out into the darkened, rear room.

I hunt through the muddle of cupboards, each lending its own small piece of jigsaw to Dennis's dreary biography. I discover that he is an unadventurous cook, subsisting mainly on tinned tuna, instant noodles and rice pudding. A chip pan sits redundant on a cooker hob caked in grease. A corner unit with a creaking hinge and a slanting door, is replete with cartons of his high calorie food supplements, clearly not to his taste but still arriving on a weekly basis courtesy of his repeat prescription. A bowl of half-eaten dog food sits in the corner, circled by flies, suggesting that the all-pervasive depression has extended across the species barrier.

I locate the Oramorph, the seal unbroken on the plastic top, and take it back to Dennis. I proffer it to him with the inducement that it might make him feel better. He responds with a question about whether it will be life-prolonging, simplistically assuming that the panacea lies in this sickly, sticky liquid. No, I say, perhaps rather too bluntly, but it will help your cough.

As if prompted, he breaks into a feeble fit of dry coughing. The dog's had enough, and heads back out to stand guard on the back step.

Dennis has yet to come to terms with his imminent fate. He can't understand why the cancer clinic has wished him well and discharged him. He doesn't see the need for all of these new and unfamiliar people dragging in and out of his house with all their paraphernalia and cheery promises. He bargains that he'll give up the fags, if the diagnosis, and more pertinently, the prognosis are rescinded. But the x-rays don't lie. Even I, with no formal radiological training, can observe the unmistakeable puffy clouds of white where there should be just black.

He's fucked alright. Dennis will depart from this depressing little abode in a coffin soon enough, with or without my assistance. Even the dog is ahead of him on that one.

With only limited means to help his master, my concerns turn to the dog. What will happen to Roly when Dennis has breathed his last and been taken away in a private ambulance? There aren't many kind souls who would accommodate an ugly, elderly mongrel who would benefit from a bath and a good brush.

I hesitate before trying to construct the question. Do you have someone to look after the dog if...? But my words peter out as we collide yet again against the awkward, inescapable monolith of his abbreviated future. Dennis shakes his head, and momentarily appears troubled, a furrowed brow appearing above his downward gaze. I decide against pursuing the conversation further and seek a way of changing the subject quickly.

I return to the sticky gloop and point to the bottle, suggesting that he tries some now as his pathetic, ineffectual paroxysm of coughing is persisting. He nods dejectedly. Yes, sounds good.

I syringe some into his mouth and as if by magic, and thankfully reinforcing my wavering credibility, he stops coughing. Cured you, I say, wishing it were true.

There follows an awkward pause, so I seize on the opportunity to draw together some departing words of wisdom and beat the retreat for another week. I reassure him as best I can but am unable to offer the words that he wants to hear; that there is another way out of this. I leave him frowning at the floor as Michael blethers from the TV to join him again next week because he's off to Quebec to meet more fascinating people.

Back in the kitchen, I encounter Roly's substantial bulk once more, sprawled out, blocking my escape route on the back step. I pat his appreciative muzzle and fondle the matted fur on his ears. We exchange a complicit glance. I'll look after you I whisper, unsure if it's yet another empty, hopeful promise synonymous with my profession. Even if you do smell of cigarettes.

I close the back gate and head back through the potholes, pondering other, easier careers. I think I could stretch to the odd train journey and inane conversation with someone dull. If only I had the wardrobe.

King of the Hill

He goes by many names, most of which he doesn't know. For a man who cherishes anonymity better than anyone, he is a popular subject of loose tongues in the village that lies in the valley below his unruly fiefdom. They don't like him; he's not cut from the same cloth.

His sepia-tinged domain is one of neglect and decay. The decrepitude is redolent of an ageing inhabitant whose grip of life is loosening. Yet he is only approaching his seventh decade. Still has a few more miles left in the tank.

He sports the unravelled haircut of a lockdown long passed. His cardigan bears the stains of meals eaten last year. The stubble on his gaunt face displays an unthreatened belligerence, safe from the attentions of any razor.

His face is set in a determined blandness that is neither happy nor sad. Ready for another day during which very little will be achieved. He stares outside through the cobwebs, deciding where to start.

Illuminated by the autumnal sunshine, the rusting carcasses of long-dead vehicles litter the muddy chaos of the garden. The mottled drabness encroaches inside a bungalow aching for refurbishment.

Apples turn brown and rot slowly in the peeling dilapidation of the glass porch. Banana skins blacken on the draining board waiting in vain for deposition in an appropriate receptacle. Teabags mount up in a grimy jar, cohabiting the space with the remnants of dead flies.

He yawns, puts down his cold coffee and picks up the gun.

A Man of Stature

They call him Slaphead. Not to his face, obviously.

He's well known in a small-town-English-way around here and they've all heard others call him much worse. They are painfully accustomed to the raised eyebrow and the shifty smirk whenever they mention who they work for.

They peer through the glass walls of his corner office watching the offending object bob up and down above the closed blinds as he conducts another animated telephone conversation. The strip lights reflect on the oscillating pink globe. They tap away distractedly at the keyboards, more for effect than with any real purpose. There is gossip in the making; it's the air they breathe.

I don't trust that slimy fucker further than I can throw him.

Why waste a perfectly good sentence when it can be lovingly peppered with beautiful invectives was Mags' motto.

Twat. She adds for good measure. *Why doesn't he work from home like the other shitheads?*

Because he wants to get away from her. Clarice knows.

Eyes meet in subtle nods of agreement. The answer is obvious.

I mean, I'm not saying that he's not a total bastard or anything, but I can't say I blame him. I mean, really, you've all met her. Abi reasons.

There is more nodding, and hefty in-breaths. Indeed they have. Juliette and her histrionics are only too familiar to them all and it would be something of an understatement to say that she's not exactly flavour of the month around here. There is still a hole in the door panel which recalls her last visit to the office.

A silence descends over the three secretaries as the strain to hear snippets of the conversation being conducted behind the glass. Words are mostly indiscernible, but his voice is low and seems to have taken on a pleading, placatory tone. They see the bald dome undulating as if agreeing with a point being made. There is a muffled but distinct "love you too" before the receiver is replaced, without venom.

Almost immediately, Clarice, who is nominally Clive's PA, sees a message pop up on her screen asking her to order flowers. Yellow ones. Those will be for Emma then.

It has been the subject of much, sometimes animated, debate between the three of them about why Clive commands such prolific interest from the opposite sex. Sartorially, his standard combination of white trainers with grey-blue chinos and a loud shirt of varyingly migrainous shades, speaks for itself. The historic facial ruggedness has capitulated to clusters of raspberry capillaries over bloated jowls and commodious double chins. His expanding paunch betrays of a man well-adjusted to the rigors of middle age and not fighting it. Conversationally he is apparently an expert on most topics, although his subject matter is noticeably narrow, and it isn't long before narrative runs dry. As for his sense of humour, well…

Hung like a donkey. Clarice opines authoritatively, allegedly without personal knowledge.

But it can be the only logical explanation.

Abi pops off for what will be a lengthy loo break, and Mags disappears into the adjoining kitchenette to flick on the kettle, scrape at her nails and check texts from her dating website. Time is dragging now that there is silence once again behind the blinds. A smell pervades the room which Clarice realises can only have come from her. She flaps her hand around ineffectually to disperse the hanging odour. Mags returns with mugs in hand, sniffs and flashes her a look which she very deliberately ignores.

Tip, tap, slurp. A dismal half hour passes and still Abi's desk remains conspicuously unoccupied.

Who's the lucky lady today then?

Henry knows damn well they're for Emma just like they all do but it's all part of his all-smiles, awkwardly flirtatious, sales patter as he schmoozes into the office carrying an ostentatious bouquet of chrysanthemums. He doesn't bother knocking these days; he knows he's onto an absolute bloody winner with Clive and as a bonus, he wouldn't mind a crack at Abi who's just sex on legs in his book. But blind to him, it's a plain fact that he's hardly God's gift, and his over-familiarity is as cloying as his easy-going manner is laboured. Definitely on the spectrum, according to Clarice. The sourness of his body odour can cut through anything she can produce; ironic for a florist they all think. Although discourse is convivial and lightly humorous, it is invariably stilted and forced, and as usual, curtailed by Clarice's hammed theatrics about being rushed off her feet. He asks about Abi as he heads out and is told somewhat curtly that she is on a break. He makes a quip suggesting that she doesn't know what she just missed before leaving with an irritated bang of the door.

Mags tuts and looks up to try and catch a glance with Clarice who isn't playing ball.

He's such a dickhead. Needs to acquaint himself with a fucking bar of soap too, spectrum or not.

She could make a prayer-offering sound angry. Clarice appears engrossed with something on her screen and doesn't respond.

Not that they've ever been asked, neither woman is really sure why they work here. There are few secretarial jobs that set the world on fire, but this one is just dire. It's only the Clive-generated intrigue that keeps them going, like being the bit-part actors in a soap opera that is constantly evolving with a plot twist every day.

The door to the corner office finally opens and Clive comes out, looking flushed. Watching porn again thinks Clarice with a certainty that has no real basis.

Ah Clarice, thank you so much.

He inspects the flowers and wears a forced ear to ear grin suggesting that everything in his world is just great. Mags gives him daggers and Clarice has to focus hard to stop her eyes from rolling and her brow frowning. He swaggers a little, searching in vain for something to say in order to lighten the mood and considers his alibi for leaving the office early. He is visibly pleased to see Abi reappear. A little more pleased than he perhaps should, as his eyes linger a fraction too long on her breasts.

Her eyes look bleary, and she wears a pale, alarmed-looking demeanour. It has clearly taken a while to compose herself.

Alright? He says disinterestedly.

Their gazes meet just sufficiently long for Clarice to notice that the query carries more weight than the single word can convey. Abi nods and returns to her desk, careful to avoid any further eye contact with any of them.

Hiyee!

They don't need to look up to register their latest visitor. This should be tasty.

Juliette strides in wearing a delusional self-confidence proportional to the level of her intoxication. A ridiculous, macabre meld of painted clown and jaundiced Barbie doll, she sports a mild perspiration having walked down rather than driven the Range Rover. She no longer bothers to make excuses. Her insight is so shot that she fails to sense the shared animosity of the room's other occupants towards her, and she cares even less. It's her baseless arrogance that really sticks in Clarice's craw.

Darling.

She sashays up to Slaphead and kisses him fully on the lips, the kind of move more in keeping for a woman forty years her junior. His expression remains blank. He disguises embarrassment impressively well but there again he's had plenty of practice over the years. He wears a convincing poker face of bland innocence.

Jules, my love. Just on my way out to meet a client...

Wisely he makes no attempt to hide the obtrusive bouquet perched on Clarice's desk.

An admirer? Juliette asks Clarice, a cold, sanguine expression darkening her face.

They're for you actually, Jules. He intervenes quickly, unflinching. The quiet background tip-tapping seems to accentuate his audacity.

He's a cool fucker that one. Got a pair of balls on him. Thinks Mags.

They're gooorgeous! What a wonderful colour, darling.

Juliette's exuberance sounds forced, more for the

onlookers than Clive who is managing to negotiate the sticky situation faultlessly up to this point.

He is grappled again and given another passionate embrace. Hands on face and an overly long mmmmmmmoaaah. The audience wonders whether they should leave or applaud.

She steps back and loses her footing slightly, betraying her level of inebriation. There is a mildly slurry inflection to her speech now they come to think about it.

Come on Clivey, how about a spot of lunch? You could spare me half an hour surely?

Darling, I'm so sorry but I'm already late. Why don't you buy us a bottle of something nice from Bijou that we can enjoy together tonight?

Juliette seems to have collapsed into him more in support of her legs than as a display of affection. She tries to nibble at his ear provocatively but bites too hard and he yells in pain. He recoils from her but emphatically manages to maintain his neutral expression.

(This is fucking priceless....) Can I get you a coffee or anything Mrs Boyce? Mags sees the opportunity for another check of her texts.

No thank you, er... A fruitless name search is being conducted through the addled grey matter. *I can see when I'm not wanted.* She juts out her lower lip as a six-year-old might when refused an ice cream.

As you wish. Mags disappears into the kitchenette anyway. Any more of this bollocks and she'll fucking vomit.

Slaphead seizes the opportunity to steer Juliette out of the office. He plants the bouquet in her hands and guides her stumblingly back out through the door.

I'll walk you to the car...

BUT I DON'T HAVE A CAR...

The door slams behind them and any further snippets of protest are lost.

A couple of phone calls come in to relieve the monotony. Mags brings everyone a brew and sits at her desk openly attached to her mobile. She knows none of the bosses will be around for the rest of the day. Clarice looks across at Abi who is clearly burdened.

What's up with you then?

A small, white, plastic cartridge is waved in her direction by way of response, the two blue lines clear and obvious.

Oh.

The neutrality of the response is all too much, and Abi disintegrates into a sobbing heap.

Shit. Offers Mags, proffering a steaming mug. *Shit, shit, shit.*

Congratulations are clearly inappropriate; they are not witnessing tears of joy here. For once, all present are somewhat lost for words. Mags rubs Abi's shoulders not really knowing why but it seems the right thing to do. Clarice takes a long slow breath. Surely, not again.

The tip-tapping is silent for a few minutes as the sobs quieten and a question hangs heavily in the air. Clarice thinks she already knows the answer.

Mags opens her mouth to make the enquiry but thinks better of it. Abi anticipates and waves her hand on a rotary motion as if parrying it away. With a resigned shake of the head and the merest of nods toward the vacated corner office, she starts crying again.

The bastard!

***

He is pumped up like a cock-pigeon, inflated by a heady cocktail of vanity and anticipation. He slams the steering wheel in a jubilant gesture of self-congratulation and admires his broad, salacious grin in the rear-view, genuine enough for a change. The addictive spice of sailing close to the wind and not being caught leaves an all-too-familiar effervescence in his chest that never stales.

Juliette's tattered veneer of sobriety unravelled rapidly as he drove her home from the office. He dumped the flowers unceremoniously in the kitchen sink and deposited her in a wailing, incoherent heap on the sofa. Without ceremony, he poured her the usual and left her with a watch-checking, tutting urgency, keen to demonstrate that her affliction had made him late. He sniggers like a naughty teenager; she makes it so damn easy for him.

Juliette's Range Rover now purrs the familiar route toward Emma's house. He marvels at his sleight of hand, his balls of steel, his delicious duplicity. For a moment he thought the girls in the office may have been onto him. He smirks lasciviously again at the thought of Abi; oh yes, she can be onto him alright. Sound enough lass that one. Unadventurous but makes up for it with her looks. She'll keep her mouth shut for sure though; she knows which side her bread is buttered.

He puts on the stereo and is immediately assaulted by a couple of bars of soulful wailing. Fucking Simply Red. He switches it off again; it's like she's haunting him. But he will not be deterred. Eyes on the prize. Never a dull moment, with or without flowers. For a man of his stature.

Ali-fucking-cante

A pungent pong hangs heavy over the stifling morass of peeling skin and sweat. The essence of stale fags and last night's Sangria is inescapable. Air conditioning, my arse.

Lumpy, uncouth youths, zombified by headphones, rub shoulders with balling toddlers. Baggy-eyed men cackle bronchitically, boasting about being out all night, comparing hangovers and bemoaning the time they had to catch the shuttle bus for this shit. Tetchy husband and wife exchanges are snarled in hoarse whispers. *No, you had the f'ckin' passports.*

Scowling dads, poised resplendently in football shirts hanging like maternity gowns, clump along in Velcroed trainers pushing squeaking trolleys piled up with suitcases. Snotty kids cast off their sandals as they perch precariously on the top. *Mummy, Daddy, look at me!*

A snaking troupe of jaundiced fake tans and tattoos, shuffle along in a disordered line, glares criss-crossing like daggers. Beneath pierced belly buttons are pregnancies that aren't known about yet. Others have developed jock itch and unexpected discharges from unmentionable places.

Beached whales in wheelchairs, bypassing the queue, are glowered at, everyone wondering the same thing. There are flashpoints everywhere. Accusations are bandied, tempers fraying; it's all simmering just below the surface. There have been chinnings for a lot less than this.

Eventually, we face the woman with caked make up, resplendent in brown and orange. She is sanguine as she repeats her script in a bored Spanish drawl.

Welcome to EasyJet. Passports?

Y Wylnos (A Welsh Wake)

It had been a dire service. Rows of sour faces wedged in like sardines on the dark, wooden pews. Only a handful of diehards knew the obscure hymns and most of the locals looked bewildered by the lesson which seemed to be in a different language again from the one they used every day to curse their sheep dogs. The cleric had clearly relished his moment in the spotlight, basking at the epicentre of what had been an excruciating hour for the rest of the shivering congregation.

The organist's arthritic fingers stumble through the minor chords of the final dirge as she contemptuously watches the congregation in her mirror dispersing solemnly towards the enticing lure of fish paste sandwiches and dry cake in the echoey hall next door. She will play a few more deathly bars until the last of them are out and then she's off to feed the cat.   The farmers and their wives divide into gender-specific groups at the first possible opportunity. The price of beef and a government inattentive to their needs are top of the agenda on one side, while the others look on sanguinely, gripping their handbags with a vice-like tenacity, observing who's looking fat and weighing up who will be next. Whispers in ears, shaking heads, sucked in breaths, and tuts.

The innate disregard for diversity resonates in their compulsion to conform. The men, with their weather-beaten jowls and pig eyes, wear short black ties over loose collars which barely reach the swollen midriff of their creased, off-white, shirts. They all wear trousers that are an inch too short. With uncharacteristic fastidiousness, they have brushed the cow shit out from their nails out of respect for the deceased. They gather in agitated huddles, great balls of hands bulging in their pockets, waiting for the cling film to be removed from the plates of food. Their women, trussed-up in dour colours and gathered in murmuring groups around the trestle tables, are united by the same hairdresser and small-minded local gossip.

The vicar appears, resplendent in dog collar, his balding head dazzling in the strip lights. He bustles around importantly, over-compensating for the absence of the family who have yet to materialise, having been waylaid at the church gate by a seismically dull, and apparently deeply affected, distant cousin. He checks his watch and wonders if the snooker will still be on by the time he extracts himself.

The air of expectation in the hall heightens as a sudden clamour in the canteen area is followed by the delivery of steaming metal teapots to the tables. The younger ones interpret this as the starting gun and they attack the sausage rolls with a farmer's hunger, piling their inadequate tea plates high. The building tension in the room palpably relaxes and the tardy stragglers start to form a semi-orderly queue from emergency exit door.

Although it's commonly held that one or two can string together a few coherent words of English, they elect not to, uniting through generations of interbreeding and belligerent indifference towards the outside world, especially to those east of the border not sharing the commonality of their language. They're keen to point out that it's their country after all, and aliens are only begrudgingly welcome. It's all down to history; centuries of oppression by the same lauding fuckers who are now the only ones able to afford a decent house in the area as a second home. The wounded natives cling to their victim status as hard as they cling to life itself.

The subjects of their ire shuffle in an awkward gaggle, uniting around the fire extinguishers near the entrance, each wondering whether it would be polite to bypass the indifferent buffet and the low-level hostility and beat a dignified retreat back to civilisation. It would only take one to break ranks and they'd all be gone. Fidgeting with the car keys in their pockets, they eye each other asking the same question.

The bereaved family eventually arrive, red eyed and rung out. There is a flurry of shoulder rubbing and formal handshaking, delivered repeatedly with a stiff, false sincerity. Cherishing their stoicism grimly, hugging is not a Welsh phenomenon.

Outside in the packed carpark, Idris and Gwyndaff squint over their cigarettes and hunch out of the biting wind blowing off the hills. They survey the cars and can tell instantly those belonging to the blow ins from their age and level of cleanliness. There is a certain degree of order and consideration for others in the carpark that is also unusual. A farmer from these parts can park where the fuck they like and be proud of it. To hell with them all.

Idris has taken a shine to one of the younger ladies serving tea and Gwyndaff ribs him about what his mam would have to say about it. He chuckles, mutters an obscenity and coughs, hawking up some spittle which is duly dispatched onto the broken tarmac.

He spots a gleaming Merc Coupe parked conspicuously across the road and calls to Gwyndaff. They wander over to stare in awestruck, whistling admiration. You can't get a ram in the back of one of those mind, and no fucking good on the lane up to your place either.

Shaking heads, they are lost for words for a minute or two before the revelry gradually evaporates into darker contemplations. Their expressions harden as the adulation is usurped by something festering that's deeply innate and they don't understand. Nor do they have the wit to express it in words. Idris feels another globule of phlegm forming on his tongue.

They are distracted by the fat perv from the Black Lion negotiating his shit-ugly dog out of the graveyard with an unsteady sailor's gait. He takes a nip from the hip flask as he waits for the dog to empty its bladder on the gatepost. His fly is gaping and the darkened spray stain on his left inside leg suggests that he has just relieved himself in a similar manner. Glares are exchanged and, had they been lip-readers, they may have spotted him muttering about fucking peasants. They're not sure if he's English, but he may as well be. He has certainly clearly marked himself out as not one of their kind. Who knew that animosity could run so deep between people who have never spoken?

Back inside, Mitch and Miriam have been cornered by the vicar who sees himself as a grand raconteur, reminiscing about the deceased's past escapades. He seems to be eulogising a different Huw from the one they knew who was apparently both funny and entertaining. They steal a complicit glance, both recognising it well enough. Let's get the fuck out of here; sharpish. Their arses have been slow cooking against the radiator as they had bided their time but the bustle around the buffet and the disappearance of the family into the seething morass of well-wishers has rendered any further detainment futile. Being pinned down by this egotistical bore while patiently waiting to impart parting good wishes to Huw's daughter was the final straw. The M56 had been a nightmare on the way over and the return trip in rush hour would be like driving through treacle.

Mitch's voice sounds tight and panicked as he checks his watch unnecessarily and offers an apology to the vicar who is mid-sentence. He suddenly feels even more like a trussed-up chicken, in his stiff black suit and stifling white collar. He pulls out the Merc keys from his pocket and waves them in the air as if further demonstrating their predicament. Miriam raises her eyebrows with a look of embarrassment and offers the vicar some warm, feminine words of conciliation before seizing the opportunity to grasp Mitch's arm and guide him firmly to the exit.

They nod in passing to the two giggling simpletons in the carpark and feel two burning stares follow them as they get into the car. From the safety of the passenger seat, Miriam reciprocates, giving them both daggers as Mitch over-revs and inadvertently wheelspins at the junction with the main road in his haste to get away. A mutual antipathy that's as deep as the potholes and sure as the slicks of mud on the roads is shared wordlessly.

Mitch flicks the screen wash and sets the wipers to remove the glutinous blob of what he assumes to be birdshit that's appeared on his windscreen. He is tight-lipped and brooding. Miriam smiles and with a warmth he couldn't muster, and a hand on his over the gear stick, reminds him that Huw was a dull but nice guy. He would have been humbled by the send-off. She's glad they made the effort.

Idris and Gwyndaff gawp at the disappearing Merc in a meld of disapproval and disbelief as it accelerates towards the brow and out of the village. Did you see the look that stuck-up Saes bitch gave you? They start laughing, remembering that Alun and his ancient, labouring tractor had just passed by, dragging the muck spreader. Within a minute or two the Merc will be firmly lodged behind it and stuck for a good four or five miles of the best road bends Wales has to offer. They slap each other on the back and cackle like fools before heading back inside in search of a nice thickly- buttered slice of bara brith. It feels like a small, but long overdue victory.

Working from Home

The dreaded piped music is playing again.

Some dirge of classical piano today which is an improvement on the usual electronic woodpecker staccato so obviously devised to provoke capitulation.

He has been rude to so many different call centre operatives from Preston to Bombay. And it's hardly surprising when primed and baited in this way. What starts out as pleasantly diverting background interlude becomes infuriating auditory torture in a matter of minutes.

Thank you for your patience. We're sorry... blah, blah.

As if there was a choice involved.

At the outset, he can happily attend to other required activities whilst the annoyance twitters out through the speakerphone on low volume. But soon he has run out of emails to delete and bank account balances to ignore, and he is back staring at the phone wondering whether or not to throw it through the window.

There is the briefest of pauses in the music, the tantalising possibility that someone may be about to answer, before the cheery refrain unapologetically returns, warbling through his fraying senses on repeat.

These are the precious minutes that he'll never get back.

And now the blue circle on his laptop revolves in electronic paralysis, the dog has started barking at an approaching Amazon delivery driver and a child has started screaming in some far-off room.

It's like pulling teeth.

There is another crackling pause before a distorted, heavily foreign accent pronounces...

Good   *******,   m*   name   is   ******, th**********ience, How *** I help?

... preceding the dial tone

And The Peacocks Strut

On the second and fourth Tuesdays of the month, the regular crowd ensconce themselves around their reserved table, prominently positioned in the front bay window of the White Hart. As usual, their booming voices reverberate around the sparsely populated bar, declaring their presence loud and clear.

They like to promenade their mantles of success, and more to the point, self-made wealth with a certain bumptious pride, mostly manifesting in the girth of their waists, the multiplicity of chins and the glint on their wrists. There is a collective satisfaction in flouncing their inflated entitlements like glittering accoutrements of rank.

Through years of practice, they have achieved a certain expertise in affecting pompous mirth and delivering stiff, offhand quips which have a tendency to sound stale and over-rehearsed. It seems to bypass them that a different world exists outside the mutual congratulation of their fortnightly soirées.

They are drawn to the White Hart, not so much because of it being the only remaining pub in the village, but because of its enticingly pretentious London prices and its ostentatious collection of so-called "boutique gins". Their positioning is not accidental; from their vantage point, they can admire the line of personalised number plates in the car park outside, declaring their presence in a similar manner to a monarch raising an ensign.

Bert, living in a sizeable mansion behind high walls a couple of miles out of the village, perpetually runs the gauntlet of drink-driving but reasons that by and large, the police know better than to pull over a Range Rover. He peers past Reg's shoulder to admire the glistening black hulk occupying two parking spaces right outside the door, enjoying the frisson of proud complacency flow through his congealing veins.

Twitchy, and thinner than he should be given the quantities of alcohol he puts away, Reg checks his Rolex for the fourth time in as many minutes. The time is of no interest to him, but he wants to be sure they've all noticed the watch. They have, of course, but no one passes comment; after all it's just another Rolex. He holds up his hand as Miles heads off to the bar and requests a glass of red wine, proper French stuff mind, none of that Californian shit. Yes, large glass please.

Arthur sits next to him, swilling the dregs of his Guinness as he once again waxes lyrical on the virtues of Mauritius where he lived for a time, working on some or other important government project. He mentions it frequently enough that they all feel an intimate connection with the island.

The ex-pat life opened doors of all kinds for him and having made more money than he'll ever need through connections and careful investment on the stock market, he likes to remind them of his good fortune by dropping passing references into the conversation revolving around the table. He's very pleased with himself generally, hands clasped over his ample paunch and a pompous smirk gracing his lips. At some point in the evening, he'll reflect once again that he never even passed his eleven plus and he's got to where is today through sheer hard graft and determination. He coughs and apologises unnecessarily, before saying that he'll need to depart earlier than usual tonight as he must get up early in the morning to take the Jag in for a service.

Attired in a country gentleman's tweed and authenticated by rich clusters of the thread veins on his cheeks, Hugo views himself as something of a benevolent Lord-of-the Manor. His handshake has a firm, Masonic grip, noted only by one other member of the company. He remains quietly hopeful that the Parish Council might consider naming a street after him on the new estate being built on the edge of the village. Repressing a belch, he remarks that his wealth manager has advised against buying equity this side of the Atlantic, the returns just aren't worth it. Arthur counters that there's no point putting money anywhere at the moment with Capital Gains being what it is, and his philosophy is to simply spend it.

Bert interjects that he is angered by the price of electricity and feels let down by the political party he has supported so generously over the years. He hasn't been able to heat his swimming pool for the past month and there is now mildew growing around its windows. His wife has put on a couple of kilos without her morning swim, he adds dejectedly.

Nodding the shining dome of his head, Harold agrees that the country is indeed going to the dogs in the certain knowledge that he can trump them all. He owns a helicopter on the local airfield and one day, he hopes that he might be able to learn to fly it. He encounters a wall of polite, but irritated, apathy when he mentions the expense and difficulty sourcing aircraft fuel.

Sensing a lack of sympathy for Harold's predicament, Miles, seating himself down on his return from the bar, changes the subject, offering the view that every one of them should own a set of Pings, it'll knock at least five strokes off their handicap. There is much guffawing and chortling to this; Miles needs to join a decent Club, or maybe come along and play in Portugal, then we'll see how bloody good his Pings are.

Miles chuckles along self-deprecatingly, in full knowledge that he'll have the last laugh over these fools on more levels than one.

After another round or two, tongues loosen even further, and the banter moves away from money onto bawdier topics. Clive, an opportunistic hanger-on, whose wallet is a poor match for his ambition, has been itching to boast about his adventurous new girlfriend, fit as you like and ten years his junior. He is about to embark on more operational detail before becoming aware of the wall of silent disinterest from his aging drinking companions, for whom sex is a distant memory, let alone how many times a night.

Sensing a brief hiatus in the sway of conversation, Miles ventures that Madeira is so passé this time of year; La Gomera is the place to head for. To a chorus of stifled yawns, he shows them his Strava profile for the week he was there recently. But it turns out that Harold took his yacht down there a couple of years ago and he thought it was shit. Couldn't find a decent steak on the whole island, and the mooring fees, well fuck me.

With La Gomera duly rubbished, Hugo expertly diverts the conversation to draw attention to his random acts of generosity and selflessness. Somewhat randomly, he drops in an astonishingly elevated figure for how much the Rotary Club made from his Garden Party event the preceding summer before shouting across an offer for some firewood to George, seated alone and coughing on the other side of the room. George, feeling suitably patronised, nods subserviently and doffs an imaginary cap.

"I'll stick it in the back of the Landy and drop it over at the weekend Georgie-boy," He receives a thumbs up from the distant corner before he returns to the group conversation. "Poor fucker". They nod sagely; he is, indeed, poor.

Seamlessly, they go on to argue about what is the best way to pass on their sizeable fortunes to their struggling offspring. The Telegraph's view, and one to which Arthur wholeheartedly subscribes, is that they'll be all the better for earning it, just like he did, and he therefore has every right to spend every penny on himself. Miles reveals that he's looking into buying a farm in Leicestershire to cash in on the Inheritance Tax loopholes. He neglects to mention his holding in the property developer who is about to submit a planning application to build sixty boxy houses on the greenbelt of the village. He'll be long gone by the time the full collective indignation is felt. And he won't be sending Christmas cards to these tedious bloody retards either.

Drying glasses behind the bar and struggling to make a dent in her student loan, Evie can't prevent her eyes from rolling as their voices get louder, their belligerence amplifying with each round of drinks and their opinions ever more detestable.

She serves Clive with a thinly disguised contempt, wishing he would stop looking at her chest. He returns a table with just a half for himself, checking his Seiko watch, "I'd best be going soon, or she'll have forgotten what it looks like!"

He laughs loudly at his own joke but despite the confident front and a fresh round of drinks, his frippery falls flat once again. He places the tray of drinks carefully on the table and stands over them, beaming like an idiot, and idling just a little too long with his skinny-jeaned crotch bulging in their eye line. There is an unenthusiastic murmuring of thanks before Reg takes a glug of his wine and remarks that he thinks that bloody barmaid has given him that Californian shit again.

Feeling chastised, and with other priorities on his mind, Clive bolts down his half and, rising from his chair with what is later interpreted as a rude expediency, departs with a half-hearted apology. Muttering the word "knobs" under his breath, he steps out into the cold with a familiar, expectant tension starting to rise in a certain over-used part of his body.

You can cut the collective disdain with a knife as they watch him disappear out of the carpark in his unwashed Vauxhall. And it's brown and fucking eight years old for Christ's Sake.

Who invited that cock anyway?

It's Harold who eloquently voices their thoughts, remembering well enough that Clive had contrived to join their exclusive club by virtue of shagging Bert's daughter for a few brief months last year. Falling in with the collective sentiment, Bert gamely denies all knowledge, and they agree to discourage Clive's future presence by changing their pre-agreed meeting day and removing his name from the WhatsApp group.

Hunched over a slow half, from his jealous corner of the bar, Rich, with his scabby anorak and half-dead whippet, shouts over an enquiry on whether the care home gave them all a pass for the night. It's all harmless banter on the surface but he winks complicitly at George who is still stricken with a cough and sits in three sweaters by the radiator, making his pint of Coke last the whole evening. Together, they chuckle along with the predictably clumsy ripostes from the window table, but the conviviality is all a double bluff; their true hatred concealed by colloquial bonhomie. George allows himself a disbelieving shake of the head as his thoughts inescapably wander to closing time and an enforced return to a freezing cold house. Rich turns back to the bar, raising an eyebrow and twisting his lips, conveying wordlessly but clearly enough to Evie his opinion of the group. She beams in agreement, as she tots up how much she's surreptitiously overcharged them over the past two hours.

Rich turns and nods to George, a gesture suggesting it's time for home, both suddenly overwhelmed by a heavy burden of bitterness in the pit of their stomachs. They are only too aware that they should have known better to come to the come to the White Hart on a Tuesday and rue their decision not to stay in and watch the snooker under a few layers of blankets.

They go through the usual superficialities of departure, bidding Evie good luck and waving hands of salutation to the assemblage by the window. Hugo repeats his promise to George about the wood but knows full well that come morning, more enticing diversions will present themselves, and all present know that promises made in sincerity under the influence of gin will be forgotten. Still, it's nice to offer.

Outside, Rich heaves on his rollie with a luxuriant satisfaction as he watches the whippet take a long, steaming piss on Bert's front wheel. He bends down as if to tie his shoelace and pulls a handful of nails from his pocket and places them surreptitiously under the chunky tyre, next to the steaming puddle. He takes the chewing gum out of his mouth and sticks it underneath the door handle for good measure.

George appears from Miles's Porsche parked unobtrusively in the darker corner of the car park, chuckling to himself about smearing his snot across its windscreen. He'd take a shit on the bonnet too if his bodily functions could be summoned on a whim.

They nod to each other and wander in silence down the hill towards the humbleness of their respective abodes, certain in the knowledge that they are sharing the same thoughts.

U-fucking-kraine

They smoke the crushed cigarettes that they've lifted from the pockets of corpses. They play cards in the sun, their hands still stained with the blood of others. Just thankful it's not their own.

They are habituated to the smells of death and woodsmoke which are a constant presence. Dogs are everywhere, hunting in packs, searching out their next roadside meal. They make for good target practice.

There is the rattle and pop of gunfire in the distance, but they don't flinch. They don't flinch for anything these days. Except insects, the buzzing reminds them of drones and of what comes next.

One has a wound that's starting to fester so they all sit downwind from him. He winces periodically but remains taciturn.

They laugh that the youngest of them hasn't had a woman yet. Plenty of opportunities here. He could practice on a dead one or a dog if he's feeling shy. There is a brief silence as they lose themselves in memories. There's no talk of home anymore; why would they self-inflict more pain?

A bottle of pilfered home-made hooch is passed from mouth-to-mouth. They grimace at the bitter burn but enjoy the brief glow it delivers. It is a short-lived, but welcome solace.

A shell whistles overhead which sets the dogs barking. They curse and shake their heads, reluctantly putting down their cards and picking up their Kalashnikovs. There is no fear, no bravado. There is nothing. They are pawns returning to the game.

Ten Letters

The dog is restive.

The man in the blue, woolly sweater with worn elbows has been staring a hole through the bay window of his living room for the past two hours. Its elevated aspect and the quality of the leather he sits on have been hard earned over the years. Even through the diaphanous film of condensation and grey autumnal murk outside, the neon lights of the city below look vibrant and stir a half-forgotten sense of excitement within him. From his vantage point the shimmering sense of movement gives the impression that the whole city below is breathing as one.

The dog nuzzles for attention, beseeching a reaction from the inanimate form slouched in the armchair. Long, silent vigils do not sit well with black labradors.

It had been the wrong time to retire.

He rubs the old dog's velvet nose, hoping to osmotically imbibe some of the apparent satisfaction the recipient gains from this simple action. His hand receives an appreciative, reciprocal lick which doesn't even begin to approach appeasing his deep-rooted sense of gloom.

Love her though he does, and unequivocally at that, he can't banish this blanket of anger and betrayal. An unshakeable indignation that all of this is at least partly her doing. This whirlwind of a wife of his; this force of nature. She had badgered him to this. She had struggled to deal with his repeated tearful outbursts in the evenings and his unrelenting morosity. We don't need the money, she had said. Think of all the other things you could do; you're not old. She said. You're young for your age. Etcetera.

There had been no disputing that her concern had been genuine and her intentions the best, but it isn't her now sitting in this sixty-year-old desolation; she is at work, being her usual self, still retaining a purpose, self-identity and respect. Business as usual.

He takes a deep breath as he has been his habit with increased frequency of late. He should have known. In retrospect, there is a great deal that he should have known.

It had been a fuck of a last six months.

The prevailing feeling as he turned his back on the sliding glass doors of the hospital had not been of intense relief as he had anticipated, but one of numbness, tinged with foreboding. There was no sense of cosy nostalgia in leaving behind twenty years of wandering up and down the same sterile-smelling corridors, wearing his white coat front, surrounded by a posse of obsequious underlings, sharing niceties with patients and duelling with an ever-revolving troupe of ineffectual managers.

The managers. Bastards. The very word raises his bile.

Some had been more human than others, but few had contributed to his working life in any appreciably positive way. Most had been contented to nibble away and undermine his authority by stealth like a slow-growing cancer. It had been a grinding war of attrition. Most of the time he felt like a bar of soap, slowly diminishing, picking up other people's detritus on the way.

No, there had never been any love lost. And the rancour grew as budgets tightened, targets became increasingly unfeasible, and he grew more inflexible and obstinate with age. There had been a growing presentiment which became increasingly difficult to ignore, but the tipping point had been the complaint and the shitstorm of accusations that followed.

He hadn't taken it particularly seriously to begin with. Like most things in his life, it had started out as a joke. He had made a characteristically flippant response to her comment about the size of his feet. He was good at flippant, cheeky, jolly chappy that he was. Had been. He was good at stubborn too. But he should have stayed more awake in the insight classes; should have paid a little more heed to the premonition that she would turn out to be trouble just from the way she buttoned her blouse. All perfume and sycophantic smiles while she mined away at his wisdom and goodwill only to recoil and strike like a viper on the basis one innocent comment. She had fucking destroyed him if the truth be told.

The dog snores gently and next door the vegan music teacher tinkles out some arpeggios on her baby grand, looking out over the same view. The lightness of the refrain suggests that the general outlook is more optimistic with the neighbours. His attention is briefly diverted from the window as he contemplates this distraction. An ironic sigh escapes him as he notices the cards of congratulation on the mantelpiece. The current frame of mind falls some way short of back-slapping pomp. Happy retirement. Indeed. Beside them the clock ticks.

It turned out that he wasn't as popular as he'd thought after all. His amiable Teflon shell dissolved quicker than his ward filled up beds on a winter night and all manner of different worms crawled out of the woodwork with axes of all sizes to grind. That's what hurt the most, those in whom he had confided, joshed, drank and laughed with, viewed as trusted accomplices, suddenly turning like sharks on the merest sniff of blood. It was as if twenty years of loyalty and self-sacrifice suddenly evaporated and counted for nothing.

Sleepless nights punctuated crisis meeting after crisis meeting but eventually after much acrimony and strong words, terms were agreed, and the complaint settled. She left with a pert arrogance and an undisclosed payment of damages, bound for some sort of high-flying academic post in a self-inflated research centre in New York, unlikely to darken the door of the NHS ever again.

Although no blame was attributed, he couldn't shake off the notion that the financial transaction in itself tacitly implied his guilt. Chastised and emasculated, every joy he derived from his work diminished and he wandered around the department in an aimless stupor. Going through the motions, nursing a grief reaction to his once proud professional career.

An occupational health assessment was commissioned, during which he spent most of the time in tears in front of an insipid-looking doctor half his age. A box of tissues was proffered to the patient side of the desk and soft words of sympathy were muttered. So began an extended period of gardening leave to take stock of his life.

His mobile buzzes in his pocket. The dog, with a brief wag of the tail, seems more interested than he is.

Another text that will be deleted without being read. Nothing important, not these days. In the distance, even through the gloom, he can still see the red lights of the cooling tower of the hospital, taunting him through the smog.

There had been a brave-faced return after a couple of months of boredom during which his garden lapsed into complete chaos and his wine rack needed constant replenishment. He limped along, nodding with fake enthusiasm to the frequent enquiries of how he was, but found it impossible to muster any meaningful level of conviction. Everything that had once been familiar felt alien.

He wasn't easy company and in the evenings that were blessed without emotional unravellings, he had been withdrawn and irritable. It had been around this time that Annie had started to propose a different future, seducing him with post-retirement delusions. He had been too impulsive, too eager to find a solution. Not in a fit state of mind to make a decision of such magnitude.

It had never before struck him how much his internal wiring had been built around his self-identity as a doctor. He had always enjoyed the patients and the individual clinical puzzles they brought with them. He had consistently put their needs above the lunatic missives from on high and petty departmental diktats, often to personal detriment. It was only natural to miss that thrill of being needed. But what had surprised him most was how much he had underestimated the need for recognition and appreciation from peers and colleagues. Only three months ago he had been somebody.

So, this beige-tinted life is now the new reality. These long, featureless afternoons. A daily list of increasingly menial and pointless tasks to trawl though. A life hollow and without meaning or joy while the rest of the world busies itself, largely unaware of his consignment to the side-lines. It would take more than swinging a golf club around a muddy field followed by a long liquid lunch to rectify this.

His limpid, turquoise eyes well up in an effort to suppress the twisting and fluctuating emotions of his private thoughts. The dog snorts in exasperation, stretches extravagantly and makes for the kitchen, yet another breathing entity feeling let down by him.

Lockdown had been the final misery. Who could have foreseen this new upside down, alien world? His plans to walk the length of Offa's Dyke with just a backpack; the cultural weekend away with Annie to Madrid, trashed and irretrievable. The world closes down in one fell swoop with a nonchalant disregard for the likes of him. Flippant it had been. That word crops up again. Bereft is another that comes to mind frequently these days.

At least the damn virus didn't trouble him. To hell with that, he would take his chances. He'd faced down scarier things in the past.

He touches the scar on his neck. The vestiges of a long past biopsy. A lymphoma. Caught in time and treated so long ago that he can barely remember the ordeal that had been chemotherapy. Derek still follows him up every few months, more out of professional courtesy than concern, so he says, but the uncertainty still hangs there in the back of his consciousness, dark and brooding. You can't polish a turd. One of his favourite professional axioms.

He swills around the dregs of the sherry in his glass.

An old man's drink. And only old men with nothing else to do can get away with cracking open a new bottle mid-afternoon on a Tuesday. He enjoys its pleasantly soporific effect. On the coffee table is a copy of The Times, folded neatly but otherwise untouched at the crossword page, the black and white squares virginal to his previously flamboyant scribblings. Ten down; pushing the buttons of low mood, ten letters.

The front door slams. Annie trills that she is home, bright and breezy in her cosy normality. He wipes his eyes guiltily and slugs down the sherry.

Her supper has been casseroling slowly all afternoon filling the house with a welcoming aroma. She throws her keys on the hall table before ghosting into the kitchen to turn on the kettle. She enters the living room with something resembling a flourish and comes over to him, simultaneously stroking the returning, wagging dog and brushing her other hand along his cheek. She smells of hand sanitiser.

"All well in Saga-land grandad?"

He nods.

Yes. All good.

Missed Chances and the Same Regrets

It still haunts me as I look up at their house. The bland, square frontage transforms into something more sinister as I recall her bruising.

The over-attentive husband admonishing her failing memory and growing infirmity. His sallow, drawn features plausible in the pedalling of lies about her accidents and falls. The stale smell of piss that ubiquitously followed her into my consulting room.

We talked across her most of the time, me probing gently, him parrying convincingly. She sat between us, gaping and mute, staring blankly out of my window.

Time has passed and I forget whether I suspected all along what went on in that dark, cluttered cottage. Feelings of guilt are almost inevitable in retrospect, but I am not proud of my contribution, or lack of.

She died first. It was the ward staff who raised the alarm to his shouting and swearing, forcibly dragging her up from her deathbed, telling her to pull herself together.

Afterwards, there had been no shortage of concerned others coming forward with their pent-up accusations. That he had been sacked for bullying a colleague with brain damage. That he had been banned three times from keeping animals. That he used to deliberately trip her when she shuffled along with her Zimmer, lean over and laugh at her, his spittle spraying over her bloodied face.

That there had been kids after all, long gone and never to return.

The things you miss in a morning surgery.

The Battle of Lidl Car Park

Conspicuous in his staple apparel, the shabby accountant shuffles self-consciously around the grimy aisles. He wears plastic black trainers with Velcro straps where there should be casual brogues. Khakis creased in all the wrong places and tucked into his sock at the back on one side. A ruffled sports jacket that was out of fashion some years before he bought it.

A Paisley cravat.

But no one here really cares. This dreary, teeming warehouse is hardly a magnet for sartorial elegance and nor is it a place for eye contact either. Bored women, baggy eyed and tired of life, negotiate squeaking trolleys precariously between the flanking hum of the freezers. Wired, edgy men in greasy overalls, grip cans of energy drinks and crisp packets, wide-eyed and looking to clock you one on the mildest provocation. Unleashed, squalling toddlers skitter between the dusty shelves like it's a cardboard adventure playground. The smell of stale fags is everywhere.

He's too emotionally barren to be a snob, but he recognises the all-too-familiar yearning to get the fuck out of this place. He's already picked up a couple of packs of paracetamol to help along her liver and he hastily fills his plastic basket with the familiar cargo from the spirits section before joining the snaking queue of shaking, cursing, tutting heads.

His troubled mood barely lifts as he re-emerges into the bleak, grimness of an insipid autumnal sun. She has been talking about stopping again and it's a worrying development. He is burdened more by the implications of this than the bulging, reusable bags which clink mutinously in his hands as he negotiates the rainbow of puddles hugging the broken curb. The brand has switched from Grey Goose to Albanian Red Cossack and although the thirst might theoretically be wavering, he's been around long enough to know that she often talks like this around the anniversary of her father's death, as if his spirit re-emerges and prods her conscience. Past experience dictates that it should only take a couple of large glasses to restore her course, and he is buoyed by an unerring self-belief in his ability to exploit her frailties, much the same as he did in his previous marriage, and the one before that.

He's already secured exclusive use of her Range Rover after she displayed the rare insight one Sunday after a particularly heavy Saturday, that she should no longer drive. Although she still views him largely as her chauffeur, in more ways than one, he knows only too well that these things change over time as the lines blur.

Take the boys, for example. After lukewarm beginnings, they embraced him a good deal more than his dress sense and social skills deserved, clearly relieved to pass on the day-to-day weight of responsibility for her wellbeing to some other brave, unwitting soul. How quick they were to take their eye off the ball and allow his feet under the table. Their complacency is now insidious, and they barely seem to have batted an eyelid to the recent adjustments in her Will. Enmeshed by the distractions of their twenty-something lifestyles, they have seriously misjudged the length of his ambition and the width of his audacity.

Bags safely deposited in the boot, he breathes a sigh of relief and starts the cautious process of reversing her Range Rover out of a space designed for a much smaller car. A skinny, dishevelled-looking man in a dirty anorak deliberately walks directly behind the vehicle setting off a cacophony of beeping alarms. The man jerks back over-dramatically, suggesting that perhaps Clive's car has made contact with his delicate frame, causing all manner of mortal damage. Seeming intent on escalation, he starts pummelling on the roof suggesting that Clive should fookin' get out and sort it. The spittle flies out of his black-toothed mouth and forms a translucent mosaic on the passenger window. Clive blandly waves and completes his reversing manoeuvre. It isn't his paintwork the man is kicking seven buckets of shit out of.

He can't help but chuckle as he drives away from the send-off of fingers in the air and bellowed insults. It is the mirth of someone who already has access to the small fortune in her current account while his adversary looks like he could barely scrape together enough shrapnel for a sliced white loaf. Her Visa card emanates a warm glow in his inside pocket. She is always close to his heart.

As he edges around the corner and nears the exit, he is moved to lower the passenger window and give the man a piece of his mind from a safe distance.

Arse!

The man, who was just about to abandon his vigil of vitriol, makes a show of extreme affront and starts to hobble, on crutches only now apparent to Clive, towards the Range Rover.

Crippled wanker!

The site of the man's infirmity has emboldened him, and he smirks pompously as he eases on the accelerator towards the High Street.

Reg Dwyer has somehow forgotten his walking stick in Wetherspoons and, as he crosses the road unsteadily towards Lidl for his weekly shop, one of his slippers emancipates itself from its fetid foot. The driver of the 168 stops in a gallant gesture to allow him to retrieve his footwear. Horace, who is driving his Seat just behind the bus, has just flown back from his mother's funeral in The Philippines. Lost in a tangle of painful, childhood memories, his blubbery cheeks are steeped in tears and thus distracted, he fails to anticipate the bus's sudden halt. Jet lag intervenes and brain and foot do not engage sufficiently quickly to avoid impact. There is a loud crunch and though uninjured, he suddenly finds himself with a lot more to cry about.

In the effort of restoring his slipper, Reg becomes discombobulated and topples over in the middle of the road, an audible crack leaves his left leg rotated at a grotesquely improbable angle. He wails loudly as a wet patch forms in his trousers. In the distance someone shouts crippled wanker.

Wayne is rolling a cigarette standing outside the bookies with the furrowed concentration of a loser. Hearing the shout, he looks up with a pugnacious jut of the chin. He won't stand for bad-mouthing the old geezers who fought in the war and made Britain great. He spots Horace's forlorn face behind the buckled bumper of the Seat and recognises the fucking foreign culprit straight away. He sticks the rollie behind his ear and strides across to the stricken car with a swagger of malevolent purpose.

The bags for the charity shop are heavy today and

Gina's spherical form needs to pause for breath halfway up the High Street. A silver Crucifix glistens beneath several chins, heaving up and down on her panting chest. She wipes her nose with the tissue from her sleeve and surveys the scene unfolding in front of her. There seems to be a blockage at the exit of the supermarket caused by some bald fool stalling his Range Rover. There's an old boy wailing away in the middle of the road, being tended to by a worried looking bus driver and a straggle of would-be do-gooders. Behind the bus, there is further commotion. Some baggy-looking chap with the demeanour of a wet lettuce is being hauled out of his car and set upon by a tattooed skinhead.

Mary, Mother-of-Christ. She pauses to wipe her spectacles, shakes her head and wrings her ringless fingers. What is the world coming to? Someone will put a stop to this needless violence in a minute. She looks again at the victim of the assault who is bent almost double against the side of his car trying to avoid the punches that are being thrown it him in a certain casually joyous manner. Even behind his bloodied grimace, she recognises Horace as the kind man with the broad smile who works at her mother's care home. Nothing is ever too much trouble for him. A sense of righteous indignation suddenly rises through Gina's chest. Impulsively, and without taking a moment to consult with the big man upstairs, she leaves her bags on the pavement and strides over to give the skinhead brute a piece of her mind. He turns and sneers at her while he gives his right hand a rest, distracted just long enough for Horace to squirm out of his grip, crawl back into his car and slam his door shut. The central locking clicks defiantly.

He's about to call her a fucking old witch and offer her the benefit of the back of his hand but Wayne recognises the woman from the food bank. The fat one with the chin hair who always slips one of his kids some out-of-date chocolate. He hesitates and nods in something resembling respect.

Sorry love.

He steps back, spotting one of his victim's teeth on the ground and slouches back across the road to the bookies carrying a faint but transient burden of shame.

Gina pulls the crumpled tissue from her sleeve, spits on it and gestures to Horace in the asylum of his crumpled Seat that she wishes to assist in making his face more presentable.

Clive is amused and distracted by the turmoil ahead of him. He hasn't considered that his nemesis's crutches are largely accessories in the claiming of disability benefit, and that in actual fact, the angry man with black teeth can hobble really quite quickly. He is brought back to the present by the rubber end of a crutch smashing into his left cheek through the open window of the car. The man's face is wild and unbridled as he screams maniacally into the Range Rover's plush interior, now tainted by its occupant's blood.

The exit remains blocked by the growing crowd surrounding Reg. In panic, Clive revs the engine and mounts the pavement crushing Gina's charity bags. A trail of freshly laundered, nearly new clothing is left in his wake as he accelerates away.

***

The blood on the upholstery has turned sticky by the

60

time the Range Rover pulls into the drive. He gets out of the car and rather pointlessly dusts himself down. His shirt is ripped, his nose is bloodied, and a black eye is forming under an egg-shaped bruise on his left forehead. But his cravat is perfect and, more importantly, the bottles are intact. Never has he felt more relieved to reach her house; he had not considered it a sanctuary on any level in the past.

He lets himself in and finds her unconscious on the sofa in front of Loose Women. There is a half-eaten bowl of macaroni cheese on the floor beside her. The small amount that she managed to ingest has reappeared and is plainly identifiable in the middle of a fresh vomit captured on the sports page of the Telegraph.

She rouses from her troubled stupor in a Pavlovian response to the clinking of glass and frowns. She has long given up on appearances. Her skin is drawn and yellow, her belly bloated. Her frown morphs into a mean sneer as she snatches the bag thirstily without a word, briefly registering his broken demeanour.

She pours herself a large one and takes a long gulp before reinspecting him with a practised, jaundiced disdain. She recoils into her viper-ready-to-strike pose.

"Fuck me, Clive. You look disgusting."

A Big Day for Christopher Robin

The fart hangs heavily in the still, oppressive air. Better out than in. Especially under the circumstances.

Dust clouds dance hypnotically in the sunlight streaming through the velvet-curtained windows. He checks his reflection in the window. A conservative Windsor-knotted tie sits perfectly centrally in his choking, pristine, white collar.

He dusts down the shoulders and lapels of his dark suit. He isn't used to feeling this nervous.

The unfamiliar, rigid formalities of his surroundings only exacerbate his tension. This clearly isn't a room accustomed to farts. The dark woods, the elaborate cornices. And the paintings. All staring down at him with aloof disdain from times long past. They knew how to intimidate back then. He feels inadequate, out of his depth, ill-equipped for what lies before him.

For distraction he reflects on his general ordinariness. Tea and toast in the mornings. A fry up at the weekend. Wiping the noses of his children. Throwing a ball for his dog. Filling his car with petrol. Buying a sneaky sausage roll from the filling station. The cheery, back-slapping camaraderie of the post-work barflies any evening in The Ship.

What he'd give to be doing any of those activities right now.

He pulls out the pack of Tic-tacs from his pocket and retches slightly as he drops a couple onto his parched tongue, such is the state of his hyper-stimulated nervous system.

A polite cough behind him intrudes his musings.

"Her Majesty will see you now sir."

The Bunker

"It doesn't bring him back."

Wise, obvious words echoing around my empty consulting room.

I find myself perceptibly shrugging as I speak them into the headset.

I realise that I am unable to find anything else to add.

A breathy, expectant lull ensues.

"We miss him so much."

There is a brittle fragility in the voice. Another silence descends. I imagine painful, shuddering sobs on the other end of the line and white knuckles gripping a telephone receiver to a heaving chest.

"Of course, of course. Take your time."

I nod emphatically at the rapidly populating screen in front of me, my textbook empathy playing out a bravado solo performance. A photo of my family smiling down from some beach in Sicily hangs above my desk, next to a yellowed MB BS diploma. The radiator on the opposite wall clanks in complaint while my scrubs dry in readiness for the smattering of face-to-faces later on. The ones that the red top media emphatically deny are happening. GPs twiddling their thumbs behind the lines again as the world dies. Etc. Standard stuff.

The lengthy silence suggests that apparently something more erudite and meaningful is required from me.

"He was a lovely lad."

This time the words stick in my throat. It catches you unaware like that sometimes. Even the most thick-skinned of medical hides can struggle to control emotions over such tragically pointless, young deaths. High as kites on ketamine, overtaking on a blind bend, their inhibitions flying out of the open sunroof. Their souls following soon after.

By all accounts it had been a gruesome scene. Hardened fireman of long service bending down and vomiting over their boots as they hosed down the blood and body parts off the road.

Innocent others had been maimed for life. It could have been my wife and kids driving home on that bend. I realise that it's fear rather than sympathy that has struck me dumb.

"Barney can't handle it. He's started drinking again."

A burn of anger rises within me. Never a helpful emotion for a medical professional. Hidden within these words is the hint of accusation. That her husband's lack of resilience at this testing time is in some way my fault. It was true that I had certainly played a necessary but unwilling witness to his various personal crises on multiple occasions over the years. Cheap red wine and vodka were his comfort blanket from a world that simply demanded too much from him. Was there ever any other way that a man who throughout his entire life needed only the flimsiest of excuses to disappear into a haze of alcohol was going to manage losing his teenaged son in a car accident?

"I'm sorry to hear that."

I realise that offering apologies has been my ubiquitous response during this depressing fifteen-minute interlude. I vary my tack.

"It must be very painful for you all. I guess he'll come out of it again. He always has before. It's

important to stay strong."

I try to inject a modicum of positivity and hope into a situation that seems as bleak as the sky outside the barred window of my room, but the words sound weak and insipid as they leave my mouth.

Outside, a group of youths kick a ball against the surgery wall. Shouting loud profanities at each other, they provide an incongruent soundtrack to the gravity of proceedings within. In another half an hour they will be buying drugs from low-slung cars across the road in the community centre carpark.

Recognising the need to draw the conversation to a conclusion I revert to my tried and tested script, preaching condescendingly that time is the great healer and there are no medications that I can give her that will relieve her pain. Dodging the obvious contradiction, I seamlessly proceed to offer some diazepam reminding myself of the magical healing powers of a prescription.

Terminating the call with a sigh of relief, I am left with the all-too-familiar feeling of impotence and uselessness. A rushed, bodged, temporary sticking plaster applied by a medical odd-job man to stem the chronic exsanguination of a rotting society. They can stand on their doorsteps banging their pots and pans as much as they like but it changes nothing in this daily war of attrition. The tiny percentage of my character that would subscribe to the Daily Mail if it was allowed wants to blame the parents.

Such thoughts normally call for a mid-morning caffeine antidote and my mind returns to the screen in silent calculation of those that could wait from those that can't.

A text from Jane arrives.

Please call Rob. Annie says he's really struggling. It would do him good to have a chat with you. XX

Poor bastard.

Smug as you like over his early retirement after years of feathering his nest through the bounty of private practice. The gloating had been good-natured but wounding, nevertheless. Within a month of dark evenings under COVID restrictions he discovers that life isn't all about status and making money.

My tetchiness has overpowered me once again. I reflect that my previously rich seams of compassion have been mined to exhaustion and I have succumbed to the emotional blunting so prevalent in my trade. I'm being unfair on my old medical school friend who has seen me through more than a few scrapes in the past. Rob is my oldest and dearest friend who would do, and indeed has done, anything for me. His generosity and warmth know no boundaries. Of course, I'll ring him later, if only to hold forth about the blue-rinsed, Crimplene-trousered generation living off the inordinate taxes of the working man.

I'm the first to admit that sleep deprivation plays a major role in my general affect but right now there is also a more profound, background, fatigue gnawing away that is proving impossible to shake off. I am lost for a cure. The rejuvenation of time away is out of the question and the weekends simply aren't long enough; this burdensome Monday morning being a fine example of how refreshed and replenished I'm not. I carry the ever-growing load of responsibilities around like the weight of my liver, viewing everything in a jaundiced hue.

It's easy to forget, behind our flimsy barricades of professionalism, that doctors have lives too. Human beings with the same baggage as everyone else. In the early days of medical school, we were told that we were part of the elite, the "top two per cent" I distinctly remember. Yet with the accolade comes a hefty burden; the tacit expectation that you are special and that every day of your working life will be remarkable in some way. That you will ride the waves of personal upset and tragedy, in the deliverance of your duties. Bullet-proof... or at least the need to be.

I am aware of the low-level panicky feeling, that was almost perpetual during my early days as a junior doctor, starting to intrude again. I'm not sure that it ever really left me but there was a blind confidence in my thirties and forties that saw me through those difficult years. Now in my fifties I have become more reflective, keen to finish my career free of reputational blemishes and avoiding the dark cloud of litigation. There's nobody here to pat my back and console me that I've done a good job or even that I've done my best. No reassurance when you're at the top of the tree – you swing on the wind in solitude.

The long, slow exhalation; an innate, physiological panacea for getting my head straight. I catch myself doing it a lot these days. Thank God that I'm way past the torture of the video training sessions of my registrar days. Right now, I wouldn't even pass 'Go'. Pleasantly torn to shreds by the tree-hugging Sub-Deans in their corduroy jackets and Hush Puppies, smiling like crocodiles as they find different ways to explain most respectfully, that my efforts were really pretty piss-poor. More open questions Dr Chase. You must seek out the patient's hidden agenda.

I look down my appointment list, the yellows

flashing to pink. I don't need to ask any questions whatsoever to second-guess the flimsily secreted agendas of this familiar parade of ingratiates. Antibiotics for the imagined infection. Antidepressants to patch up the unhappy marriage. A request for a battery of food allergy tests to paper over inadequate parenting. The demand for assistance to prevent procurement of a bottle of vodka after breakfast every day. Write a letter to tell an employer detailing the litany of imagined medical reasons for being lazy, sloppy and work-shy. The expectation that since the same conversation last week I have miraculously managed to find a cure for ageing. A missing bag of controlled drugs, left on the bus again and an abundance of tittle-tattle medications queries, mostly recurring. And the unrelenting apologies; that the NHS is so woefully underfunded and under-staffed that it cannot meet your needs, that the world is too cruel and uncompromising for your delicate disposition and of course that I wasn't born with a halo and wings and that I am, in actual fact, a mere mortal.

Loneliness. Lost love. Inadequacy. Addiction.

I recall no lectures in medical school on these staples of my every working day. No diplomas awarded on how to drag people out of the fetid mire of mostly, self-generated misery they live with. Senior lecturer in Anatomy carries more academic clout than Professor of Pure and Applied Self-loathing any day.

Case in point, next on the list is my regular weekly circular conversation with Rita, a pleasant lady in her seventh decade who, when sober, vaguely reminds me of my own mother. She will cackle, wheeze and slur down the line before she embraces her real agenda of firstly requesting yet another referral for detox followed closely by a plea for benzodiazepines to fill the stopgap. Her son is back for Christmas, and she somehow needs to miraculously present herself in a better state. I occasionally enjoy a little banter with her when time permits but I'm not unrealistic about the general lack of progress medically. She will end her days miserably, and nothing I have to offer will alter that bitter truth.

A fight has broken out in the carpark. The shouting has become more urgent and uncouth as arms and legs flail around unimpressively. I reach to speed dial the police in the expectation of no response once again but in the short time of my contemplation, it's all over and there is a rapid dispersal as an Audi A5 with blacked out windows pulls up and pauses briefly to talk to one of the combatants. There are nods of ascent, a certain definable tension in the air, and within a minute the car park is empty once again.

The town has plumbed new depths when it is largely policed by its own purveyors of torment. Doubtlessly the same people whose sick notes I sign month-on-month. The uniqueness of my position in the society of middle-English drabness doesn't make it any less depressing.

I am shaking my head again, in sure knowledge that my time for coffee has well and truly arrived. It has become apparent that this will be yet another day when I won't be saving the world. I will muddle, dodge and weave my way through the next few hours and come 6.30 my armoured invincibility will dissolve away, leaving my long-suffering family forced to tolerate what's left. The early doors large G and T followed by the silent supper. The long soak in the bath during which I will feed my morbid fascination with the obituary page of the BMJ. A few sleepless hours in bed anticipating the day ahead...

Sorry.

Sunday Morning Single Parent Club

The dog crouches down, lifts its tail and looks at me almost apologetically, that we must undergo this steaming ritual once again. If he could, he'd buy me a pint later. I pull out the polythene bag and do the necessary.

From behind the wire mesh fence, a child in the playground remarks to her father that a dog has done a poo followed by a *bleuhhh!* of disgust. He doesn't respond, being too absorbed balefully dribbling a ball, fixed on his phone screen.

He looks rough. Last night has clearly taken its toll. Stubbled and a scowling, he wears the stern, indignant frown of worldly rejection. It's his turn for the girl today and his ex had insisted on an early pick up, more out of spite than necessity.

On the far side of the playground, a woman wearing heavy makeup is hunched in the hood of her anorak texting with one hand and vaping with the other. Her fingers are tattooed rather than ringed. The content of her empty buggy has been dispatched and is hurling himself like a dervish from one scrappy bit of play equipment to another, unwatched.

There is a ping on the man's phone which he briefly consults before lifting a smirking gaze towards the woman. She meets his eye with a look of wry complicity on her face.

He gestures towards the graffitied bench.

A tryst is made over a can of Red Bull.

I walk away, sniffing my fingers.

Duck's Arse

Yeah. Hurt like fuck, both of them.

The orange-skinned, leathery man stinking my room out is a coiled spring of antagonism. He's referring to his knees. They are bilaterally rather painful, apparently.

He winces, scowls, then rubs them both simultaneously to emphasize his point.

He deliberately uses the F word to demonstrate his scant respect for my professional position and to assert his deeply rooted conviction that all doctors are privileged, pretentious arseholes who know fuck all about the real world.

He holds his hands out in front of him and cracks his knuckles impatiently as if urging me to not piss around. Under his tattooed forearms I catch a glimpse of the line of scars tell-tailing on his adolescent experimentations with a razor blade. He catches me looking and a darkening in his eyes urges me against probing further. As if.

He has a pockmarked, brutish, instantly dislikeable, face and I have to remind myself of my long-departed mother's axiom of not judging a book by its cover. I relax my shoulders and try to focus on viewing him in a more positive light.

He has made an effort in his appearance to attend the appointment today. His camouflaged shorts have carefully ironed creases, and his white vest is pristine. Curly hairs from his weathered torso explode chaotically from underneath it, conjuring up images in my mind of a chimpanzee. Knuckle-dragger is a phrase that inexplicably inserts itself into my consciousness.

He has clearly doused himself in enough of Poundland's finest aftershave to sink a battleship, presumably with the purpose of laying a fragrant diversion from the stale smell of fags on his breath.

His hair, greying slightly with the snitch of a nicotine patch over his forehead, has been ruthlessly backcombed and Brylcreamed into the shape of the proverbial duck's arse. He is bejewelled from his teeth to his fingers. A chunky gold chain menaces through the forest around his neck while the sovereigns on his fingers gleam seditiously for the want of a nice juicy jaw, like mine, on which to imprint themselves. His teeth glint like his pig eyes, lending to a general demeanour of extreme untrustworthiness. Another axiom about all that glitters comes to mind.

It can be a struggle sometimes, this positive attitude thing.

His hands, for all their gold glorification, are gnarled and callused. I've already guessed before he answers my enquiry about what he does for a living. The building trade takes no prisoners. I suspect they've done their fair share of fighting over the years too. Some of the tattoos on his left forearm are rudimentary enough to be self-penned, perhaps in the long, solitary boredom of a prison cell. Five dots, a Swastika pointing anticlockwise, some faded initials of a past, now forgotten, liaison.

With precision interrogation, I wheedle out that he has spent the last week laying paving stones without pads and both his kneecaps display the ensuant pink swellings, the size of hard-boiled eggs. He doesn't look kindly at me when I suggest the possibility of housemaid's knee, so I hastily amend my diagnosis to a more masculine bursitis. Still fighting a rear-guard, I explain how it's come about and that, given the choice, I'd take that over osteoarthritis any day. I'm sure that I manage to reassure without being condescending, but I could be wrong.

Whatever his past story, I can see that the years weigh heavily on his embattled body, and it won't be long before other conversations will be had about the wear and tear of his joints, the emphysematous chasms in his lungs and the furred-up blood vessels choking his heart.

I offer what I perceive to be the sweetener of a sick note and am surprised when it is rebuffed with some vehemence in his rough, rustic manner.

If I don't work, I don't get paid.

He makes the point like I should have known all along and was imbecilic to suggest it. His face displays a brief glower of bar-brawl readiness, accompanied by the merest jab of a gilded finger. He may as well have added the word "dickhead" as a sign-off. This is all going swimmingly.

He is clearly expecting me to pull the proverbial rabbit out of a hat. Patch him up good and proper, and he'll be gone, leaving the reek of cheap aftershave hanging in the fetid air of my consulting room for the rest of the week.

I pause, delving deeply into my depleting reserves of patience. I explain that his problem won't go away anytime soon unless he rests up and for that, there is no short-cut. In particular, he must desist from any activities that involve kneeling.

Open-mouthed, he fixes me with another confrontational stare suggesting an edge of affront. He's decked people for less than that, for sure. His assertive glare seems to enquire of me what I think he might get up to with his mates on a Saturday night. I'm pretty certain that it will involve drinking buckets of lager, standing up presumably, until they fall down. But I wonder again how long he might have spent inside, and what they might have done to him there.

I have wandered yet again into unhelpful, negative conjecture about him and I privately rebuke myself. I am about to propose the tried and tested escape route of a prescription when he catches me off-guard.

As you brought it up doc, I have got a bit of a problem down there...

He gestures towards his genital area, a passing wink of a beady eye, a momentary flash of the teeth.

What sort of problem?

Well, you know doc, the kind that crops up on a Saturday night.

Another half wink that's difficult to interpret but may indicate the merest hint of embarrassment.

You have impotence?

Yeah, that's it, doc. No joy at all. Whatever I get her to do...

... I think it's my prostrate.

He says it in a way that implies it's all my fault before proceeding to volunteer a few crude and unnecessary examples when his unfortunate appendage has let the side down. I nod sympathetically, pitying his poor wife. We continue to talk in code for a minute or two until I feel sufficiently cornered to reluctantly offer an intimate examination. He rises off the couch, shaking his head, and makes for the door.

Nah, fuck that. No one's sticking their finger anywhere near my hole.

His point is made as categorically as it is coarse and

I acquiesce, perhaps a little too readily, to his explicitly expressed wishes. I rather flakily propose the compromise of a trial of Viagra which seems to appease him, the whole, glorious hidden agenda of his visit revealing itself in an instant.

I take the opportunity to throw in some futile advice on the evil effects of alcohol and smoking on that particular department but it's only too apparent that he's not listening and is hungrily awaiting the printout of the panacea. An awkward silence ensues, whilst my archaic machinery splutters, clicks and flashes, before eventually obliging.

Limply, I try to revisit the original point of this consultation and offer some bland, obvious suggestions for his painful knees. But it's clear that his mind has wandered on to more pressing matters like his mates waiting in the pub, and a cold frothy pint sitting on the bar with his name on it. And a wife at home, safe in his current incapacity, about to get the shock of her life.

It's the end of the afternoon and I'll be as glad to see the back of him as he will be of me. I tell him if he's quick he might just catch the pharmacy next door before it closes. I open my door in a gesture that some might construe as politeness but with the dual purpose of reminding my adversary that our business is done, and he can now quietly fuck off. He leaves with a barely appreciative sneer, a cursory "cheers", and the distinct absence of any real gratitude. I watch him strut down the corridor back to the waiting room in a manner suggesting that he owns the place. "Piece of shit." I call after him. In my dreams.

I reach into my bag and pull out the nearly empty plastic water bottle that had started the day replete with neat vodka. I neck the dregs and pop a couple of Extra Strong Mints as a chaser, dousing my hands liberally in the double bluff of alcohol sanitiser, before turning off my computer and following the trail of cheap fragrance towards the exit.

There are a smattering of staff remaining in the reception area and I relay my usual jovial goodbyes from behind my face mask, sucking hard on the mint. Outside the sun is low in the sky and still bright, disorientating me momentarily, having spent all day under artificial lights. I search my pockets for the car keys, surveying the bird shit on the roof of my beaten up Astra.

A pristine white Porsche Cayenne rolls past, leaving the surgery carpark. It slows down in front of me, ensuring that I notice, and I'm graced with a gold-glinting thumbs up as it passes. I catch a glimpse of the registration plate as it revs around the corner.

B19 MAN.

Quite a car, eh?

I am joined by Julie, our ever-effervescent reception manager, who like me has made her escape from the mayhem for another day. I hadn't put her down as a petrolhead. Before I can reply with something judgemental and probably inappropriate, I discover that she is already on first-name terms with my new favourite patient.

Old Ernie's a one, isn't he? Getting his knees in that state laying tiles in his pool on the Algarve. Should know better, a man of his age, she admonishes with a certain levity that I would find difficult to muster.

She clearly knows a lot more about his predicament than I had bothered to uncover. In light of the new facts presenting themselves, the spiteful, frazzled, end-of-the-day-and-get-the-fuck-home side of my brain wants to reconsider adjusting my diagnoses once again to safe-breaker's knee and crack-dealer's droop. I find that I like him marginally less than five minutes ago.

Disconsolately, I chug off in the Astra, setting a course for Lidl and replenishment for my water bottle.

Stirring My Brandy with a Nail

Stirring my brandy with a nail.

He wished he could remember who sang it. Such a great line. All these years later it was still a memorable snippet from that trip.

He couldn't remember if it had been a CD or a cassette, nor the Volvo or the Toyota. But it had struck a chord with both of them at once and sparked an animated conversation that had lasted nearly thirty miles.

There had been something about its delivery that had smacked him in the face. He would like to hear the song again, if only he could remember. There were a few other things about that trip he would like to relive; remember better.

It had been the last time that he'd seen her. Lain with her. Exchanged intimacies that were bilaterally about to be transferred to others.

Overall, the weekend itself could not have been considered a success. It had been their swansong. Neither had been keen at the time to frame it in these terms but both knew that their lives were moving on and difficult decisions were beckoning. The necessity of a final mutual analysis had become pressing.

It wasn't as if either had disagreed with the other's appraisal of their combined long-term outlook but there was a tinge of sadness as they parted outside her flat. Polite 'thanks' and 'see yous' that never materialised.

Maybe it's best not to recall who wrote the song. Press delete on the whole thing.

The Mourner

He cries.

It isn't a whimper either. It is a primal, guttural noise wrenched deep from his throat. It signals that he is going to occupy many more minutes of my day than I can afford.

He has messed up the tissue paper covering on my examination couch. It is crinkled beyond the perfect flatness I had concocted prior to his arrival, and I feel mildly perturbed by his carelessness. I remain silent, suggesting with my twenty years' experience of body language that it's his turn to talk.

Yet he wails on, making no attempt to articulate the particular source of his misery. I peer at the pharmaceutical company clock on the cobwebbed wall above his head. Its battery is running flat and it's ten minutes slow. Even so, it suggests in real time that I'm already overrunning by fifteen minutes.

And now this.

Being masked, I hope that my eyes aren't betraying my growing feelings of exasperation. I offer him a tissue from the box, diminished by over-use. He takes it with an appreciative nod, blows his nose violently, and inspects the product in seeming wonderment. Finally, after a few deep lungfuls of air, he manages to sufficiently gather himself to string together a few coherent words, one of which is an apology.

I enquire how I can help.

He mops his eyes with his sodden paper ball and pulls out another tissue from the box that I left at his side, unbidden.

When he starts talking in a rough, local accent, he is

more articulate and loquacious than I had expected. It is as if I am the gatekeeper for his emotions and through the simple offering of a box of Kleenex, I have allowed the trickle to become a tsunami. The words come flying at me.

It's his wife. She died. Four months ago. I gather that she had been desperately ill on a multitude of levels but still it appears to have come as a complete shock to him. He was the one they asked when they needed to turn the machines off. Sixteen years together. He loved her more than life itself.

He pauses and I start to formulate the best way to ask him why he's decided to come today of all days to ask for help. Before he continues, unbidden.

He is lonely. He is bereft. He showers infrequently and hasn't used a toothbrush for weeks. He is living on slices of plastic, white bread with something processed in between. He is drinking. Heavily. He has thought hard about the point of carrying on. Every day, in fact. He manages, just about, to carry on his monotonous duties in a factory because it's a distraction and a reason to live. But only last week he nearly had a fight with a colleague over who's turn it was to make the coffee and is now facing awkward interviews with superiors. He throws in that he frequently feels a tugging pain in his chest; an aside which I choose to ignore. It seems irrelevant in the general context.

The second hand on the wall rotates lethargically. He wants me to turn it back six months. And make everything right.

I am framing the best words to repeat the question as to how he feels I can best assist before he launches into another torrent of words.

He has no joy left in his life. He has no one to talk to other than his two dogs who I am appalled to hear sleep in his bed with him every night. Yet for him, sleep remains elusive.

His sister is perpetually on his doorstep, cajoling and badgering him in equal measures, but still, he can't find a way to open up sufficiently to tell her how he feels. Not really. He comes home from joyless factory shifts and works some therapeutic grime under his fingernails, dabbling with his motorbike, just to delay opening of the first can every night. But there's only so far that these menial acts of maintenance can stretch, and ultimately the pointlessness of it all is overwhelming. He is currently on two four-packs a night.

I miss her so much.

And he's off wailing again.

I know there'll never be anyone else...

There is an ECG awaiting my attentions in the nurse's room. My computer screen has taken on a life of its own as it lights up in pink, the new late-in-the-day arrivals awaiting nuggets of my wisdom. A message flashes up; a nursing home is requesting an urgent visit for a resident who has lost consciousness. There is an impatient rap at my door which I ignore. It's difficult to focus a fatigued and fogged brain when it's being bombarded like the Donbas.

I glance at a picture of my departed daughter on my desk. There is a resolve in her young eyes that helps me to feel grounded.

I have to move this along and intervene at some level. It seems appropriate to start at the beginning, by explaining to him about the grief reaction, pointing out that it's a process that needs to be worked through and for him it's early days yet. The guilt and the hopelessness are typical. Understandable. Normal. But they will pass. And at some point, he will start to feel better, and life will move on.

He frowns at me, unconvinced by my sage words. It's beginning to look like a prescription for antidepressants is going to be the only way I'll get rid of him.

Then he tells me that it's her birthday tomorrow and off we go again.

I glance again at the clock which, not only subliminally suggests the name of the drug I should prescribe him but also tells me that my life has just lost another ten minutes which I will never get back. I glance back at the picture of my daughter again; if she could, her head would be shaking in the same way that his is, but for different reasons.

My patience is straining to accommodate the burden sitting in front of me, selfishly shedding his moisture into my consulting room. This annoying man who has crow-barred himself into my burgeoning duty surgery, messed up my pristine couch and worked his way through my box of tissues. He appears to feel that he holds the monopoly on misery and grief. I want to tell him that I barely see anything else, day in, day out. It seems that he hasn't considered that he may not be the first person to wrestle this slippery adversary.

These are tense moments, and I need to tread carefully. One false word and I will be accused of being callous and uncaring.

Ok, look...

I clasp my hands together, summoning all the resources of resilience, experience and sincerity that my jaded thoughts will allow.

We need to consider this from your wife's point of view. What would she say if she were here now?

He pauses to look at me, a glimmer of incredulity on his face, and momentarily I think I've lost him completely.

He blows his nose again and seconds pass in his silent contemplation. Eventually, he volunteers that he hadn't considered that angle previously. We have apparently reached a point of reluctant epiphany.

It's true that she had disapproved on numerous occasions about his reliance on alcohol to deal with "bumps in the road". She had been a roll-your-sleeves-up-and-get-on-with-it type, and it turns out that she would almost certainly have taken a dim view of all this gratuitous wallowing in misery and self-loathing.

I need to pull myself together.

I nod. We're here to help you.

***

Outside on the sterile, vinyl seating of the waiting room, Mrs Norris fidgets and makes a show of looking at her watch again. Her bladder burns like razorblades and if they keep her waiting much longer, she'll be late for her weekly prayer group.

The young man sitting next to her with a sunburnt, shaven head has apparently just walked in from a building site. He shakes his head sardonically. He is ugly with indignation.

They couldn't organise a piss up in a brewery, this bunch of clowns, could they? He sneers.

She nods, not really sure what he means. There is a red LED message board on the opposite wall imploring patients to continue wearing masks inside the surgery. She notices the young man wears nothing but filthy clothes, bulldog tattoos and a belligerent grimace on his bristly, red face.

I've been waiting forty minutes to see Dr Chase... She volunteers,

And then instantly feels bad for what she regards as a potentially mutinous comment.

He lets out a prolonged gasp that could be a very elongated "shit".

Like ah say, bunch of fookin' clowns.

She nods again, a little hesitantly, suddenly unsure on who's side she is on. Dr Chase has always been so kind to her, and he is a very busy man. Everyone knows. With all that's been going on. It's on the news almost daily.

Her doubts are heightened further when the man suddenly lunges out of his chair with a certain pugnacious purpose and heads, in a wide-armed swagger, towards the reception desk on the other side of the room. Whatever she has said or done certainly appears to have triggered him.

Her hearing is bit off so the specific details are lost in the echo chamber of a waiting room, but there is nothing wrong with her eyesight and she can see banged fists, jabbed fingers and the pale, nodding face of the girl behind the desk who barely looks old enough to drive.

He turns back onto the waiting room with an easily audible "fookin' joke" and kicks over a leaflet stand to emphasize his point. It falls with an unexpectantly resonating crash and now everyone's attention is on him.

In a brief interlude of lucidity, the man seems to realise that he's made a complete arse of himself in front of the small smattering of stragglers in the dying light of the late afternoon waiting room. Embarrassment denies him the recourse of sitting down again so the only mildly dignified option is to leave, which he does with much head shaking and repeated 'fooks'. He spits on the floor and boots the door on the way out to demonstrate his general disenchantment with everything.

A young, tired-looking woman on the far side of the waiting room shakes her head and seems to chuckle to herself behind her mask. She has been there an hour, trying, with only limited success, to keep her grizzly, shit-smelling toddler occupied. She picks up his dummy from the floor once again, sucks it briefly herself in a misguided act of hygiene, and coaxes it once again into his bawling mouth.

Something about her reminds Mrs Norris of the times when she took her own kids to the old surgery on a Saturday morning to see Dr Stallard. Smelling of whisky and all done up in bow tie and waistcoat, he used to make them all wait while he finished his cigarette outside. But in the musty, leather interior of his consulting room, he gave them his full attention for as long as they wanted and always with a reassuring, warm smile on his lips.

She looks around at the slick lines of décor, the white, neon strip lights, the hand sanitisers everywhere and the posters of domestic abuse helplines; things have certainly changed over the last thirty years.

Over the top of the shining laminated reception desk, Mrs Norris notices with alarm that the young receptionist is crying. Muted, shuddering sobs. The abuse she absorbs every day is cumulative and the latest vitriolic words imparted have all been too much. She is about to go over to the girl and offer some encouragement when she hears Dr Chase's booming voice echo down the corridor as he ushers out a miserable-looking man who, despite his general demeanour, is in fact faintly smiling. They shake hands and something unsaid is exchanged. She sees a gratitude etched into the man's face as he walks away with a certain levity in his step.

Dr Chase, looking almost alien in a mask and polythene apron, addresses the room in general with a sincere but tired apology about keeping everyone waiting. Formalities over, he turns to her specifically, a recognition between them spanning two decades, and gestures her up the corridor towards his consulting room.

Mrs Norris, how lovely to see you. I think you're next?

Her aged heart palpitates momentarily. What a lovely man.

This Door is Alarmed

Indeed.

Its shadowed eaves have born witness to all shades of humanity. From the peeling paintwork of indeterminate colour, a weather-faded sticker of Che Guevara looks on in stout admiration.

Spat gum congealing on stilettos. Tights laddering and knees grazed as hasty, gagging blow jobs are administered to the smirking bouncers. Shaven headed and pugnacious in their black polyester, stinking of last week's perspiration.

The drunken, fumbled, gropings under skirts barely substantial enough to wipe a nose. Underwear strewn as necks are bitten. Urgent new alliances yet to exchange names. The discarded condoms splattered against it.

Whispered words, and furtive exchanges of cash for substances secreted in places where no self-respecting substance should find itself. A nod and a wink, a bump of fists. Until next time.

Bent double by the violent spewing of guts. The chaotic spray of stomach contents mixing with the lipstick dogends and maggoty pizza crusts on its meandering path to the gutter.

The all-pervasive, rank stench of stale piss, nonchalantly sprayed into the dark recesses of the graffitied wall, while others desperately queue inside for the dysfunctional toilets.

The brutality of boundaries crossed, and bitter scores settled. The shattered teeth and crunch of bones. Spatters of blood decorate its scarred panels, chipped and broken by bricks thrown and heavy-booted kickings.

The same familiar paramedics scraping up another

bloodied punter off the grimy, cobbled backstreet, never to return to the hedonistic neon hubbub of Dino's Bar.

The door's not just alarmed. It's fucking petrified.

Gone

It had been one of those crisp, green Autumnal mornings that nudges the senses how good life can be. A low sun dappled through the swaying branches. Birdsong was audible above the uncouth growl of the diesel engine as he drove the familiar route into work. Unusually, he was replete with optimistic anticipation for a bright day ahead. Warm-humoured and cheery, he would put right the ills of Edgecombe and return home along the same familiar road, bathing in the glow of achievement. An ordinary man brimming with good intentions and pretentions of greatness.

Three hours later, it just happens to be another unexciting, run of the mill, Thursday morning at Clay Lane Surgery. No dramas, no lives saved, just the usual minor crises on repeat. All very humdrum with a peppering of teeth-grinding.

He finishes a phone call with a man of mature years who seemed most perturbed to be told that the pain in his hip might just be arthritis and a function of his age. His irritation turned on Dr Chase for his impertinence, as he tried to bargain himself away from the diagnosis with childish boasts of athleticism and high activity levels. He was clearly uneasy and unwilling to be acquainted with the processes of aging; nor compromise for that matter, indignant that his overpaid GP hiding behind the barrier of phone triage, must surely have something up his sleeve. His much-repeated view was that a scan would put everything right. Something must be done.

The gulf between want and need. Another staple that Dr Chase was never taught at medical school.

He is, for once, content that his bright blue scrubs are commodious and more fitting for a man three stone heavier and six inches taller. His desk fan isn't working, and in the oppressive heat of his featureless, cuboid working space, he feels only mildly uncomfortable. He is blissfully unaware of the thin veneer of sweat building on his forehead and the tell-tale earthy waft emanating from his armpits.

The earpiece allowing him to converse with patients hands-free, like any other self-respecting twenty-first century GP, catches on his spectacles as he throws it on the desk in a fit of resigned despondence. The positivity of his early morning commute has evaporated and now he is plagued by the constant, familiar niggle of things undone. A general feeling of disharmony with the rest of the world clings tenaciously to his conscience.

He has become accustomed to feeling tetchy and bored at work. This bloody pandemic feels like a millstone from which he will never be free. Every day, contradictory directives from on high rain down on him and it's taxing trying to relay advice that's as perplexing as it is constantly changing. He is apparently expected to have answers to questions that no one in authority has even yet considered. The patients who watch the morning news know more than he does. *You're the doctor,* they keep saying.

The enforced isolation of virus-dodging seems to have led many to decide that their children have ADHD, and their bastard partners are just shit people to spend any time cooped up with. Every gripe has bubbled its way to the surface, and he is expected to supply remedies for all.

He decided within the first crazy month of mayhem

that the narrative of a plucky NHS wrestling down the viral foe was not for him. His younger colleagues may have signed up to it in their naïve enthusiasm, intoxicated by their newly discovered status and respect, storing up tales of COVID heroics to recant to their grandchildren, but he would have preferred to have just sat this one out. The option was never offered.

There had been clapping and banging saucepans on their doorsteps again last night. It wouldn't take long for the tide to turn and for all this selfless sacrifice to be forgotten. He's been around long enough to know that. Never had he yearned so much for a good, straight-forward case of constipation.

He is strongly in need of the pep of caffeine to drag him through to lunchtime. All morning his mobile has been buzzing and now is his first opportunity to catch up. He slips it into the pocket of his baggy blue tunic with the intention of catching up in the hoped-for solitude of the staff room and puts on his mask in preparation for the journey. It's tedious having to tog up just to walk to the lavatory, but rules are rules, and everyone is taking it all very seriously. He rinses yesterday's coffee mug under the cold tap, swills it around with his finger a couple of times for good measure, then heads out into the virally laden menace of the corridor.

He bumps into his senior partner by the patient's noticeboard and is relieved to find that he isn't actually the most miserable man in the building. Dr Meadows has a good twenty years of moaning under his belt and trumps him every time for cynicism, pessimism and sheer dreariness. Today, he is on a mission to bellyache to anyone he can corner about yet another factually inaccurate article that has incensed him in today's

Telegraph. Dr Chase listens patiently for a while, making polite sounds of general agreement, before his innate survival sense kicks in and he excuses himself on the limp pretence of a sick patient awaiting his ministrations. Sometimes Meadows is absolutely the wrong person to meet in the corridor.

He moves through reception, dispensing muffled, masked greetings and words of cheery encouragement to the fraught staff. But he is careful not to tarry, thereby avoiding the snarl up of some inevitable minor query.

Without further incident, he reaches the relative sanctuary of the staff room which he is only allowed to enter if there are no more than two people already in there. He peers through the porthole window of the door and is relieved to see only the trainee, Seb, alone and hovering impatiently over the kettle. He enters, and after the usual salutations, they do a little cat-and-mouse COVID dance over the milk, one having to wipe it down and leave it at arm's length on the work top for the other to collect.

Bespectacled and erudite beyond his adolescent looks, Seb is easy company to sip coffee with. He possesses an enviable self-confidence and boundless enthusiasm that haven't yet been eroded by years of patient defiance and NHS bureaucracy. There was a time when the practice would have attempted to lure him as potential future partnership material, but he has already made it abundantly clear that there isn't a hope in hell that he's looking at anything involving long-term commitment. He only has to look at the state of the partners.

He's sorry to bother but has a couple of cases he needs to discuss, so once again, Dr Chase is distracted away from the buzzing, pinging object weighing down his pocket.

In the cupboard under the sink, they find some date-expired biscuits which they decide to eat despite the obvious risk of cross-infection. They leave a trail of crumbs over the sanitised surfaces and swap some Netflix recommendations before eventually returning to the pressing questions which need answering. Suggestions are made that it isn't always sensible to continue lowering a ninety-two-year-old's blood pressure as the learned boffins in their academic ivory towers would advocate, before Dr Chase finally remembers his hyperactive mobile. There are four missed calls from Jane. A text flashes up, "Annie's just called. Rob's had a heart attack. I'm going over".

He reads the message over several times more, unsure if this is some kind of joke, but gives no serious thought to the possibility that, only a few miles away, a medical emergency is in full flight on the kitchen floor of his best and longest friend's elegant townhouse. He imagines Rob is chuckling away on a gurney in A&E, a drip in his arm and a few leads on his chest, sweet-talking the nurses and appealing for two biscuits with his cup of tea.

He excuses himself from the persistent Seb and tries to return Jane's call but there is no answer, and he is left hanging. What now? He is paralysed by indecision and a pang of panic ripples through his chest. Despite working for the NHS for the whole of his career, he remains a man uncomfortable with the feeling of being out of control.

He rings Jane again and leaves a message for her asking her what he should do. Then he texts her calculating that one or other will prompt a response. He is about to pass through reception again on the way back to his room when he is called to one side by the practice manager who has been lurking in ambush.

William is a good sort, keen to paper over the widening cracks as best he can. He fixes Dr Chase with a searching, paternal look and smiles affably. Historically this usually means bad news as indeed is the case today.

He has just completed a lengthy phone call with another irate patient. It took him four days to obtain a phone appointment and then all Dr Chase could suggest was that he was old and needed pain relief and rest. His neighbour, a prominent and esteemed private sports therapist, insisted that the only way forward was through a scan.

He shakes his head in disbelief and emits a few mild expletives, a reaction with which William is all too familiar. He calls after the disappearing doctor, telling him not to worry, he'll straighten things out; it was just for information. He'll catch up later.

On the way through reception, the flimsy elastic of his mask breaks and his staff are graced by a glimpse of his long-forgotten bristly chin and a mouth that's chewing lemons. The expression on his face is familiar enough to them and they all know well enough to keep their queries to themselves.

His room seems to have heated a few degrees in his absence, and he flops in the chair suddenly overcome by a stifling exhaustion. The phone is buzzing again in his pocket and in his fluster and fumble, he manages to turn to it off instead of taking the call. It's Jane again.

He calls back, camouflaging fear with an affected, casual, nonchalance.

What's going on? How is the old bugger?

Her voice is thready and quiet, but it reverberates around his box like the chop of a guillotine.

He's gone.

Gipsy had always been a maverick. She likes to demonstrate her uniqueness by writing her name on things, sticking her gum on door handles or displaying her bum from the tops of buses. Even her name, bestowed on her long before her wayward tendencies had seen the light of day, suggested how events might unfold.

Dreamt up by her spliff-smoking mother while listening to Fleetwood Mac. It had been a king-size and a double album and by the end, she had also acquired the middle names of Moonlight and River. The initials of the local radio station. Funny.

Who could have thought it would lead to this?

There is still blood under her fingernails as she fidgets with the dull, chipped laminate of the custody room table. She'd really like to look him straight in the eye, but the invisible force of intimidation fixes her gaze to the scuffs on the floor.

He wears a practised look of resignation. Over the years he has worked hard to affect a demeaning disinterest in cases like this and these days it all comes very much as second nature. He mouth-breathes through uneven lips. His belt has missed a loop, and his shirt has escaped on one side giving him a skewed, asymmetrical aspect.

He wonders if he'll manage to keep a straight face on the name thing. Cracking his knuckles, he picks up the single A4 of her scrawled statement and waves it in her face.

"So! Miss Fantasy-Marigold. Is this just going to be litany of unredacted expletives?"

The Extra

He has been briefed.

He takes a moment or two to compose himself. The senses of irritation and indignation that this woman has chosen to impose herself upon him at the end of a taxing day need to be suppressed and compartmentalised well away from the next few minutes. He reminds himself that this is the life he has chosen and in the worst-case scenario he is likely to be delayed by no more than an hour from the drivel of evening television.

He takes a long, deep breath before clicking the icon on his screen that summons her from the waiting room. He consciously drops his shoulders in effort to relax.

The noxious reek that catches her draft as she enters the room does not bode well and provokes a primitive response deep within. Once encountered, never forgotten. The unforgettable waft of death stalking.

She bids him a perfunctory hello and turns to the boy of around ten who is still holding her hand. She bends down, a little too closely into his face, and cajoles him to wait on the seat outside the room, a comic and a packet of Rowntree's Fruit Pastilles serving as the apologetic compensation. He nods obediently, wordlessly.

There is a robustness about her as she sizes him up, meeting his gaze with a certain defiance. A calculation is in motion as to whether he will be malleable enough to collude with her rationalisations and not let the side down. He has spent too many hours sitting in this featureless room, and seen too many like this, not to recognise the fear behind her veil of pallid boldness. He gestures without words to the chair beside his desk and concentrates hard not to betray his rising sense of doom.

It's difficult to put an age to the woman, she has strange, unnaturally flat hair which he suspects is a wig and her face is anaemic but otherwise featureless. Assuming the boy to be her son, he takes a guess that she is around forty. Her record, flickering up on his computer screen, confirms that he has over-estimated by two years.

They have not met before, and she has arrived in his consulting room at this belated hour via the circuitous route of an aborted duty nurse appointment. Her story to the reception staff had been sufficiently vague to not to call for the ministrations of a doctor. His colleague had realised within less than a minute that this was way out of her league and so here she was, a malignant extra, added onto the end of his bulging afternoon clinic list. A note from the nurse pings up on his computer screen. *Brace yourself.*

She starts with an apology because it's probably nothing and just a waste of his time. She had sat with it for a while because it almost certainly was unworthy of bothering a doctor. She can't remember exactly when she first noticed it but it's only over the past few days that she'd noticed the blood in her bra. She stares at him levelly whilst divulging this information. There is a hint of confessional in the way that she talks. Her pupils are dilated but otherwise there is little to suggest any reciprocation of the growing foreboding that he feels. Her conscious mind has clearly over-ridden her visual and olfactory senses. She appears unperturbed, matter of fact even.

Outside the square concrete walls of the surgery, the evening is darkening, suffusing a neon glow through his semi-closed blinds. The estate kids have started to knock a football against the wall of the surgery, as is their nightly ritual; an annoyance at the best of times but under the current circumstances the imposition seems greater, almost violating. The incongruity of the gravity inside with the careless, youthful frivolity externally is grating.

He apologises for the circumstances beyond his control and, wearing an expression of sincerity, tells her that he hopes he can put her mind at rest. He smiles and she responds. Perhaps we should have a look?

Sure, of course.

He pulls the blinds tightly closed and notices the wince as she removes her cardigan to reveal a dark, blue shirt that is stained around her right bra cup. The shirt buttons are undone with shaking fingers, and she wrestles to unclasp the bra, finding that it has stuck to her breast. He shudders to observe her discomfort as she exposes the craggy, offensive mound underneath.

It is worse than he had expected, much worse, and he is briefly lost for words. An irregular dome of purulent slough now inhabits the space between them. The breast, as an entity, is unrecognisable, the dusky skin ulcerated, fungating and oozing blood. The stench of decay is overwhelming. It is as if the right breast has checked out from the rest of her body and has decided to putrefy all by itself.

A less-experienced man would have baulked, struggled to disguise his revulsion. But the twenty battle-hardened years as an NHS GP that have eroded and left a shell of the man he once was, have simultaneously nurtured a stout resilience, an ability to take even the worst of circumstances in his stride. Not for the first time he uses the computer screen as a diversional crutch, checking some spurious details from her medical past, the main enquiry hanging pregnant in the foul air between them. He tries out the words from several different angles.

How long and why?

She volunteers that, as far as she can remember, she'd noticed the first discomfort over a year ago. Her breasts had always been a bit on the lumpy side, and she hadn't thought much about the increasing nodularity. She makes no mention of smell or appearance, as if her brain has closed down certain sensory channels in misguided self-protection. On reflection she thinks that maybe she first noticed the blood on her bra a couple of weeks ago, but it had taken a while to get around to booking the doctor's appointment. Life is busy. She pauses, a little embarrassed. Surely, he must know how difficult it is to get through to the surgery on the phone. It's like a fortress, she jokes.

She hesitates and suggests hopefully that perhaps she may have an infection and needs antibiotics.

He tests his cautiously neutral tone for fit and finds that it emerges as condescending.

I mean, it's possible. But there are other things to rule out first.

He checks for her reaction. No offence appears to have been taken and she is shown towards the examination couch where she tentatively lies and braces herself.

He dons rubber gloves to examine her, in truth giving himself a little breathing space to decide how to approach this spikey matter. He does not want to touch her breast even with the protection of latex.

Her armpit is replete with engorged lymph glands, more inhabiting the triangle of pale flesh above her right collar bone. On closer inspection, the white strip lights of his room reveal a yellowing of her eyes. He prods her abdomen with a measured concentration. There is an unmistakable fullness in the right side concealing an unapologetically rugged liver.

He pauses, theatrically removing the gloves and washing his hands. This brief hiatus allows thinking time. Right at this moment, his brain is a vacuum and difficult words hang in the air, just out of reach. She struggles to reinstate her clothing, carefully arranging her cardigan to conceal the stains on her shirt. They sit and face each other and for a few seconds, sharing a weighty silence.

The diagnosis is beyond doubt, and there's no way that he can dodge the issue, but he will employ every slippery device he has perfected over the years to avoid mentioning the almost certain prognosis. Not his place. He will leave that unenviable task to some unfortunate oncologist. He had not signed up for this all those years ago, motoring pints in the medical school bar.

It is a challenge to look her in the face, knowing what she conceals within her baggy clothes.

There is a faltering in his tone as he tells her that, in his opinion, things don't look good. He studies her face for a reaction as she readjusts her bra. He awaits the arrival of tears, but they remain absent as she steadfastly maintains a neutral expression. She knows; but won't allow it to permeate through her thick skin.

He continues that he thinks it's likely that she has breast cancer and that the best thing to be done now is an urgent referral for further investigations. The C-word is out of the bag.

She nods, swallowing hard but still her face remains inscrutable.

Okay.

He waits for more words and a couple of breaths pass before he realises that this is the sum total of her response to the seismic pronouncement he has just dumped. He is not a man for small talk at the best of times and now he finds himself utterly bereft of any further meaningful comment.

Good.

The word is so inappropriate, he wishes he could retract it as soon as it's spoken.

I'll just get the nurse to tidy things up for you ...

He nods towards his white-light bolthole.

He emails the nurse and blocks off a couple of her appointment slots for wound dressing. He is heavily burdened by an inescapable feeling of futility. Her boat has long since sailed and it is now just damage limitation. The why question still lurks unanswered.

It is clear that she carries a deeply rooted stoicism that will not be daunted by his spoiling words. He wonders about her internal dialogue, wishing he could conjure up something that might somehow improve the dire situation. His mind wanders to estimating just how large a gin and tonic he can pour himself on a school night.

Finally, he stops the clumsy tapping on his keyboard and looks up to tell her it's all done. She thanks him for his time and his honesty, looking him in the eye, the merest hint of moistness in hers. He enquires who is at home and she replies with a faint shrug. My husband. Apparently, that is the name he goes by. Much could be inferred from how long this has gone unnoticed.

But she is keen to steer conversation away from even more difficult areas and smiles at him in contrition. It must be a difficult job, she observes, telling people things they don't want to hear every day.

Her directness is disarming and her candour humbling. He has spent most of the last week moaning about damned, bloody patients wasting his time and now this one person for whom he might have made a real difference if he had seen her months before, is beyond his help and offering him her sympathies.

He nods. It can be.

Her bravado is weakening, and she has spent enough time in this awful, brightly lit space in the presence of this kind, but odd man with his bad news, beer paunch and garlic breath. She has a yearning to escape; hide under the covers in solitude and wait for it all to pass.

He estimates they have finished, having exhausted every awkward avenue of conversation and stands up to open the door for her.

Is there anything else that I can help you with?

She hesitates and gestures for him to pull the door shut for a further moment.

How long?

He suppresses the impulse to shrug and opens his palms to her, sucking in air through his teeth. It's impossible to say. These things are difficult to predict. It's really important to stay positive.

She nods in acknowledgement of simple truths and thanks him once again for his time. She opens the door to leave. In the corridor beyond, he glimpses a scared-looking boy, unacquainted with the art of remaining blind to what's in front of his eyes. Their stares meet briefly before he is whisked away down the corridor towards the waiting room, an odour of decay hanging in their wake.

The boy's name is Crispin. He is bullied at school because of it. He will be briefly reprieved in a month or so when they all hear of his mother's death. And he will regret that he didn't talk more to her about it while she was around.

Zakynthos

I'll never come back here.

This ugly edifice poking ungainly from the turquoise shock of the crystal Ionian waters.

Where the ubiquitous bleached dust, the custodian of the blood and bones of real and imagined armies over centuries, metastasizes itself into every crack and crevice.

Where they pretend that they have no English but still charge you for the privilege.

Where they nonchalantly desecrate their rich history and ancient olive groves with a sea of plastic detritus.

Where old men with leather skin stare you down on the potholed roads, from their decrepit mopeds, their eyes communicating more than anything they might mutter under their tobacco breath.

No wonder they hate us; the tattooed, peeling lobsters and pudgy lard-arses staggering around the all-inclusive strip party-on regardless. *It's all free mate.*

Amidst the neglect and chaos, the swallows and dragon flies dive-bomb over the pool, and a proud man presides over his ancestral domain of verdant vines on a child's bike. A man of warmth, culture and learning, he is the one saving grace in this dustbowl of malevolence. But even he doesn't stay, opting for the familiar, frenetic bustle of Athens when the summer ends and his guests leave. And he is old; the last of his kind and will play no further part in shaping the future of this place. He knows his die is cast.

I'll never come back here. A conscious choice rather than the latent threat of time passing.

Fucking Zakynthos.

Six out of Ten

He's close. The grey shroud of death lingers menacingly over Joe's haggard features. His previously vibrant eyes stare into the middle distance, occasionally fixing on me with what may, or may not be, a meaningful stare. His mutinous lungs heave on manfully, like a failing bellows around the unrelenting cancerous mass, strangulating in his chest, soon to snuff him out. But he's not ready to go yet. In a final act of defiance, his vital functions press on against the odds.

In an uncharacteristically emotional moment, he let slip last night to one of the twilight nurses that he is petrified of this grim inevitability and not yet at peace with his fate. A sad admission given the certainty of the predicament. Obstinate to the last, left to his own devices his death will be an unnecessarily drawn-out distressing affair for all involved. All eyes point to me to settle this conundrum.

I am met at the door by his wife, puffy cheeks stained by tears and a familiar pleading countenance in her eyes. A few quiet words are exchanged during which I ascertain that the overall situation is not good. Desperate in fact. The bags under eyes and the limp, flaccidity of her skin testifying to the amount of sleep she's had in the past few days.

I find him camping in the dim light of his lounge, the monstrous hulk of a hospital bed occupying half the room and happier times from his life staring down from the walls.

There is a flicker of recognition as I greet him in as cheerier manner as I could muster under the circumstances. His eyes are open but dull. His body is emaciated and as close as it's possible to be to being dead while his heart beats on. The family dog sits with him placidly, seeming able to offer better comfort than humans or any of the pharmaceutical armoury I have to offer.

I take his hand and search fruitlessly, for some ember of new inspiration before embarking through my usual list of futile enquiries.

How are you doing?

Deservedly, he doesn't answer, gentlemanly opting against some of the four-letter responses that would emerge from my mouth if our roles were reversed. He takes a long slow deep inspiration which seems to more or less articulate his position.

Are you in pain?

He shakes his head and confirms that currently, pain is not part of his dying process.

Is there anything that I can do for you?

He fixes on me again with a gauzy gaze which seems to strongly suggest the urgent need for release. *Give me all you've got.*

His brain stands impatiently by the exit door, but his heart and lungs confound his wishes and want to party on. He shakes his head listlessly and responds with a polite but exasperated 'no'.

The dog, a smiling retriever, licks my hand as I simultaneously hold Joe's. We sit in silence for a few awkward moments. I want to excuse myself from this pointless exercise but at the same time realise that this is probably the last time I'll see him breathing. And maybe it's not pointless to him.

A dismal, silent futility descends upon us, neither of us knowing how to break it. Moments pass. In the hall, a grandfather clock ticks ironically, as if mocking the fleeting nature of the human condition. The possession of warm blood and a beating pulse is temporary.

The dog is uncomfortable with the silence that has descended and wags its tail impatiently, imploring some attention. It's clear that we all want this to end. I'm conscious that the onus lies with me. The simple act of opening the door and walking out.

I'm appalled to hear myself say the words "take care of yourself" as I stand up to leave, as if I'm advising him to eat a little less cheese and take more exercise. But I've only been doing this job for thirty years and I've yet to work out the appropriate phraseology for this drama that has played on repeat throughout my career.

Goodbye Dr Chase. Thank you.

His words are croaked and weak, but the emotion is strong. He seems genuinely grateful for my paltry ministrations. We shake hands weakly for a final time.

Outside in the hall, his partner is grim-faced and expectant. She corners me by the ticking clock in anticipation of wise pronouncements.

I don't think it will be too long.

I judge that this is obvious and my saying the words might come as something of a relief but instead she sheds all vestiges of forbearance and crumbles into a chaos of tears. I feel moved to put my arm around her, something I generally try to avoid in all its awkwardness. She isn't unrealistic; just not ready to hear it articulated so starkly yet.

She detaches herself from me and wipes her cheeks with the back of her hand, shaking her head. I'll be alright she says unconvincingly. We move together into the kitchen where a hospice nurse is poring over paperwork and checking ampoules.

Some family friends flutter around, trying to be helpful and unobtrusive but only emphasizing their presence by doing so. Well-meaning people, lost in the maze, like the rest of us.

Joe's wife leaves me with the nurse. I am a little surprised to see that she is wearing a full uniform when many of her palliative care colleagues seem to have opted for more comfortable, informal clothing. We have not met before, but I can see by the way she intently studies the drugs and charts that she is from the stickler school of nursing rather than the touchy-feely type.

She looks up and introduces herself as Jill and I realise that we've had several email conversations about Joe. We exchange platitudes, offer our viewpoints on how everyone is bearing up. No, we agree, it won't be long. I suggest notching up the doses a tad before checking my watch. I need to get back to the surgery, I explain, feeling a little like Judas.

I move to the front door where Joe's wife reappears. I tell her, not for the first time, that I'm sorry and ask hollowly if she's okay. She responds politely in the affirmative, both of us brushing aside her convenient lie.

Outside, the Honda belonging to the family friends is blocking me in and they make something of a song and dance about the simple acts of finding keys and reversing.

While I'm waiting for them to move, I reflect on whether I'll ever meet these dying souls again in an afterlife, be it up there or down below. God, and the other, knows, there have been enough of them over the years. This conveyor belt of humanity for whose departure I have been responsible overseeing. I ponder what feedback they'd give my general contribution to their closing moments as they relinquished their slippery grip of the mortal coil. The firm handshake and the nod of appreciation, or the cold shoulder and averted gaze? Six out of ten maybe? Perhaps this will be my own epitaph, come the day.

But I don't dwindle on such esoterica; safely ensconced in the dusty mire of my Vauxhall Astra, my mind flits back to the present and whether I'll buy a chicken or beef Ginsters from The Co Op on my route back to the surgery.

Life goes on.

Two Men

Well, what do you think?

Huh?

What do YOU think?

I pause for a moment, not sure what to think.

I look at it again, and it confirms that I really don't know.

I shrug and make horse lips, hoping that this may be a sufficiently evasive response, only to be met by an expectant and malevolent silence.

Well... I venture.

I kick it and scratch my chin in my best approximation of a perplexed frown. I'm not sure how I had become so misdirected as to be in this place, with this person, in front of this thing.

I mean, you can't fuck with it can you?

He offers his opinion with a gold-toothed sneer and a hefty dollop of venom. I can smell the bestial tang of his armpits. Menace exudes from his every pore.

I sniff. He has a point.

Mean old bastard of a thing, eh?

It is.

I nod and pass a cursory '*yep*' to fill the silence.

In fact, I reckon it's a complete cunt.

He enunciates the syllables of the final word with a provocative glint in his wicked little eyes. His whole demeanour is a balled fist. He's testing me.

I nod in deference to his greater knowledge of such things.

I thought I wouldn't like him and so it turns out. I need to terminate this through my prodigious reserves of stealth and guile.

I study his mean features and pat the wallet in my back pocket as my flagging fight or flight rolls and tumbles across the space between us.

So... how about we talk over a pint then?

Sais
(For K.J.J.)

Aside from the casual racism, it was the dismal autumns that melded seamlessly into the brittle, harshness of winter that grated with her most. The levity of her spirit visibly wilted in the unrelenting drizzle of the short, sunless days. The depleting reserves of misguided optimism which still lurked after being the first in her lineage to be the proud owner of a red brick Bachelor of Science degree, evaporated as the first October storms lashed in from the Irish Sea.

The wet, gun-metal slate of the roofs, the oppressive, granite drabness of the buildings and the dirty, rainbow puddles of the potholed roads all seemed firmly ingrained into the dour psyche of the locals. Generation upon generation of hard, uncouth people, forged and united by adversity. They harboured grudges as others might collect stamps, effortlessly wallowing in their joyless existence.

In the featureless town, the pubs brimmed with men shaking their heads, stoically supping their flat pints. Some railed, some fought, but all bore their misery with a tacit resignation. At home, in their staid two-up, two downs, their gormless kids gawped inanely at repeats on TV, while mousey wives hid away, slack-jawed in darkened back rooms, basked in the misty cocoon of cheap sherry or barbiturates.

Perched precariously on the edge of civilisation, the town relied heavily on the geographical umbilical cord of a decrepit and unreliable railway. There were three tortuous, incoming road routes, but few travellers stopped to tarry. It was a place to pass through, mouth a few derogatory words, and move on to somewhere else with a foot firmly to the floor.

Although it was a topic that she quite deliberately never pondered for too long, she would like to have known more about what it was about her that automatically asserted her position as an outsider. There were of course, a few obvious differences that set her apart. The wide, looping vowels of the Wirral Peninsula betrayed her origins when spoken amongst the clipped, harshness of the local dialect. Through marriage, her elevated societal position was doubtless the source of much local chagrin. Hitching herself to one of their own who had travelled to the city for his medical degree before being unceremoniously swept back into the fold. Each native carried a chip on their shoulder deeper than the valley itself and there was an unmistakable reticence in the widely held local knowledge that his thriving medical practice had been gifted to him through familial benevolence. The privileged son of rich farmers from another valley, parachuted through blood ties to assume the role of Their Doctor. The embers of dissent may have burned but Idris's shortcomings through birth could be easily mitigated; for he shared their language.

Over-arching everything, was history. The simple bitterness against centuries of injustices that translated into an innate antipathy to anything English. The old scars ran deep and could never be healed by something as facile as her warm smile and easy manner.

She personified the enemy.

Or was it because she was a woman? A wilful, attractive and educated one at that, who was incomparably superior to their own pinched, miserable, conniving betrothed, huddled together on the High

Street, voices hushed, deriding anything or anyone they felt threatened by.

The malign started casually enough, and indeed, her sharp Scouse wit had stifled a laugh in the realisation that she was being blatantly ignored in the local bakery. She had waited patiently behind two dowdy women with tight perms while they gabbled in their native tongue to the woman wearing a pink house coat behind the counter, apparently impervious to her presence. A lesser character would not have confidently strode forward and intruded into their conversation with a beaming smile and a polite "excuse me?" But in itself, this simple act, marked her out. She left with a loaf that was already a day old and a certain reputation for audacity. English too.

It didn't take long for the already narrow minds to further close. She became an outcast almost overnight and her deficit in the language was soon to be weaponised against her. The shopkeepers seemed to slow deliberately to attend to her. She soon found that goods bought through the medium of English frequently paid a premium. Racism and discrimination were not words in common parlance in Sixties Wales, but she became all too acquainted with the word *sais* whispered behind hands, with its subtle derogatory connotations. It was easy to draw comparisons with other words, used in similar circumstances, by other peoples, that could result in a lynching.

The feistiness of her character which had elevated her from a lowly working-class childhood, living in a post-war, prefabricated bungalow to a university degree with honours was not yet completely exhausted and, with the weight of her husband's growing professional reputation behind her, she applied for a teaching post at the local comprehensive. Over-qualified though she was for the position of head of biology, the handicap of the language barrier followed her like the smell of muckspreading, and she was begrudgingly employed only for the want of any other, more local candidates.

Idris's medical career had taught him to approach spikey problems head on, so on his recommendation, she strode into her laboratory on the first morning, looked every member of the assembled rabble in the eye and said clearly and loudly, "*Bore da*".

It was a simple enough gesture but served its purpose admirably in winning over the ramshackle group of farmer's boys who could barely spell biology, and whose only prior knowledge of the subject had been restricted to watching the sheep rut. *It's the lead in the water* as Mrs H would later remark.

Winning over a smattering of the duller-witted kids was only remarkable as being small victory in the context of a raging World War. The elevated bubble of the staff room turned out to be divided along similar lines to the rest of the town, and there were only a few brave souls who crossed it with the delicate olive branch of friendship.

Mrs H, a brusque, no-nonsense Lancastrian, had seen it, done it and wore the badge in her eight torrid years as the head of English. Eyes and mouth like razors, she bore the multitude of insults with a certain resigned grace. 'They don't know any better,' she would frequently repeat, a scattergun statement broaching a broad palette of ignorant slights.

Harris French's bronchitic cackle reverberated through the corridors as much as his bellowed reprehensions. His wicked grin flashed in a glimpse of jaundiced nicotine. He was as Welsh as they came, but having lived in Toulouse for a time, he maintained a somewhat broader perspective, and more liberal attitude to the world as a whole. He liked her spirit, the general cut of her jib. He could see that she was different, in more ways than the obvious, and that her time in this primitive backwater would be a hard one. They forged an unlikely friendship and through his acquired wisdom and acute knowledge of the local politics, she found a renewed sense of purpose and blossomed in her new circumstances.

It was soon after her first miscarriage that she changed.

Neither she nor Idris knew how to manage the whirlpool of emotions in the goldfish bowl of constant scrutiny. Both were now well-known, if not necessarily liked, local faces and generated no small amount of gossip. It was an impossible place to hide. A silent sadness descended over her that felt every bit as weighty as the leaden skies above. She no longer felt a willingness to indulge the townsfolk in their petulant, spiteful games. She discovered an unexpected rage brewing against their pathetic parochialism. She could no longer simply laugh things off.

The following year, the birth of her first liveborn should have been a welcome epiphany but early signs were not positive. Mr Griffiths, the benevolent, bushy eye-browed headmaster, made it clear that he didn't expect to see her back at work until her daughter had started school herself. On face value, the gesture was exceptionally accommodating in its generosity for, like Harris French, he too had fallen under her spell. But unintentionally, it also severed her lifeline to normality, extinguishing any remaining spark she retained.

Motherhood was not something that came naturally in her late thirties. Long days on her own with an unsettled baby only served to inflate her sense of isolation. Her litany of differences effectively excluded her from the various covens of young mothers in the town and her despair grew. He would arrive home from a long day of listening to other people's woes to be presented his screaming daughter at the door as she disappeared, eyes to the floor and coat in hand. In the quiet solitude of a walk by the river, the imagined conversations that she had in her head with the chief persecutors did nothing to lift her feelings of hopelessness.

During his frequent trips to the tobacconist, Harris French's jaded gaze noticed her grimly pushing the pram around town and he worried for her. He, more than anyone, knew how her rediscovered identity had been carved out through her work in a laboratory smelling of methane, and the winning over of hearts of a few ignorant young boys. Now that it had been removed, she was like a boat cut from its moorings, at mercy to the raging tides. Sometimes they talked, focussing on the old days rather than the present, but the rapport never reached its previous conviviality and like everything else, the friendship drifted.

In silence, her anger grew like a cancer. The frequent, tetchy arguments with Idris often escalated rapidly into all out shouting matches. The brief solace of the over-employed gin bottle solved nothing.

Against the odds of her biological clock, another daughter arrived, effectively ruling out any hopes of a return to her profession.

While they were young, it was easy to lose herself in the anonymity of the children's needs. Attention was diverted away from her, as the doctor's spoilt brats usurped the millstone moniker of the doctor's wife at the tip of every gossip's tongue.

As her first-born reached school age, she also hit the all too familiar barrier of prejudices. No milk or toilet absences unless requested in Welsh, with all manner of minor affronts following. The prejudices of the parents merely passed on to their children like history repeating.

The all-seeing eye of Harris French did not need to look twice to know that she was lost. The waste of human potential was too much for him to bear witness. Even from a distance he could see that she had surrendered herself to a superfluous life of kids' parties, inane Tuesday evening whist drives and mind-numbing charity work.

Twenty years passed in dreary normality. One after the other, her daughters lurched through their bigoted education and, feeling like second class citizens, wasted no time in heading off to a university east of the border. Idris's arteries, congealed by a childhood of high fat Welsh staples, finally capitulated and he keeled over without any final words of import after one particularly hefty January evening surgery. An avalanche of sympathy cards followed, the majority with sincere condolences written in Welsh.

Finally, she had been handed a ticket to escape. There was nothing to compel her to stay other than a nice house and a certain historical popularity with aging farmers. But her courage had dispersed along with many of her friends from English side of the border and the thought of starting again somewhere else at her age proved too much.

So, she stayed and aged in tender togetherness with a labrador of increasing girth, the one being in her life who did not judge her for her language, or lack of it. Slowly her mind softened, depleting the fighting spirit that had borne her through so much, descending her into a dotage of apathy.

And now, the girls visit her grave periodically. She is buried with him in the damp, dark clay on the outskirts of town. The inscription on the headstone, in a quiet corner of the cemetery, is worn by the weather and sits next to that of one Douglas Harris which bears the words, *Vive La Différence*. Even ten years after her death, there are farmers slouched over flat pints in the Black Lion who will tip their glasses to her memory with wistful grins.

Sometimes, when they remember, the girls will bring flowers, but more often they are empty-handed in the knowledge that it will be many months before they return, and there is no one else to clear the dead heads. They pause, for a few moments of damp contemplation to pay gratitude to them both, but never for long enough to ponder the true depths of pain and sacrifice.

And they don't tarry. They make sure there is always somewhere else to go.

(Author's note on Welsh text: *Sais* – literally means "English". In certain contexts, it is regarded as a derogatory term. *Bore da* – good morning.)

The View from the Window

So, it appears that the world hasn't fallen apart. Not quite, not yet. He finds it reassuring but also a tad disappointing.

And he's sure they haven't forgotten him; they just haven't called in a while. His phone still works, and he checks his voicemail daily.

And the days aren't dragging at all, they just seem longer, less frenetic, more evenly paced.

And his friends only rib him in a kind and gentle way because he is of a certain age and disposition, not because he's newly retired and his grip of reality really is loosening.

It's true that the gears of his brain do indeed grind a little sluggishly at times these days, but in a good way. Pruning roses triumphs over crunching spreadsheets. And a few minor lapses in memory do indeed occur, but it's mostly the frivolous trivialities of arguable consequence. And what's important is that the small daily chores that used to ignite the frisson of domestic tension are now slowly getting done, generally.

And the way his wife pats rather than holds his hand is in no way patronising, and no less tender.

And the unique lightness of each morning is not lost on him because he now has the time and space to allow his mind to drift and dance through the splaying sunbeams and over the chattering birdsong.

And the view from his window is a pleasant one. Why shouldn't he spend more time admiring it?

The Lucky Man

The rancid atmosphere in the Evans household has benefited little from the medical misfortunes of its main breadwinner.

The Sergeant's stroke proved not to be fatal but left him with the burdens of hemiplegia and an inability to speak in anything more than repetitive, barely comprehensible grunts. His trademark scowl is now confined to one side of his porcine face while the other twitches and dribbles limply.

Had he been able to effectively communicate his extreme rancour about the circumstances, he would have spoken less about the apparent permanency of his physical afflictions and focused on the helpless misery of being entirely dependent on his wife's ministrations.

Given the frailties of their pre-morbid relationship, it had been widely expected that Sergeant Evans's future would have been firmly sealed on discharge from hospital. Long term residential care with the odd cursory family visit; bunches of garage flowers and gift boxes of Maltesers, which he wouldn't be able to eat. No one was more surprised than he when his previously disinterested wife stepped forward and volunteered with an apparent selfless altruism to tend to his every need.

And so it is. His days pass in dismal, pyjamaed, tedium.

By contrast, she has started to dress more imaginatively since his arrival home. Her figure, previously camouflaged under layers of baggy pullovers and loose-fitting tracksuit bottoms, is now fully on display for all to study its every last voluptuous contour. A cleavage has suddenly appeared and is proudly displayed most days. She manages to find a multitude of reasons to bend down in front of him, revealing glimpses of parts of her anatomy that have been out of bounds for longer than his damaged brain could recall. Her hair now has a certain shape and sheen that draws attention, a clear change from the mousey, straggled, drabness of his healthier days.

His mind moulders and curdles darkly as he imagines the attention she garners when she's out of the house on her increasingly frequent errands. The whole town knows of his predicament and there are many he knows who would gladly offer her a shoulder to cry on. And the rest.

She's started talking about someone called Clive from her evening art classes. Not to the stricken figure of her husband sitting in the piss-smelling wheelchair directly, but around him, within earshot. The words "sensitive", "supportive" and "compassionate' are exhausted by overuse whenever Clive is mentioned in revered tones. The district nurses who visit know him alright, a bit of a lad apparently. There's a running joke about how erect he likes his easel.

The contractures on The Sergeant's left side seem to tighten and burn when the C word is repeated once again, sometimes whispered over his catheter bag change, others while offering a cup of lukewarm, milky tea carefully placed just out of his reach.

She's a salty one alright. New exotic fragrances waft over him as she changes his sopping bib. Somewhere deep inside, forgotten impulses stir in a catheterised body part that is best left alone. She wears a gloating smirk on her face that communicates all he needs to be reminded about how the balance of their relationship has changed of late.

"Bisch!" He offers.

She returns a serpentine smile that says "fuck you" much louder than she could ever speak the words.

"Bisch!" His defiance has pathetic pluckiness. She pats him patronisingly on the side of his face he can't feel and shrugs her shoulders hard as if locked in a permanent giggle.

***

The district nurse visiting this morning is middle-aged and wears the worn look of resignation synonymous with her profession. The pristine creases of her starched green uniform cannot mask the unwashed body beneath. He can tell from her manner that she dislikes him but can't place precisely why. There may have been a disputed parking ticket somewhere in the dim and distant past.

She is tight lipped, economic with words, knowing there will be no reciprocation as she washes him with rough efficiency. Get on with it and onto the next job.

She checks his catheter and flushes it, the chore she seems to enjoy most. She rolls him to the side and checks his bottom for sores, finding an area that starts her off tutting. She tells him that he's lucky she's spotted it and slaps some greasy cream onto the area with all the sensitivity of a blacksmith before manhandling him back into his wheelchair.

Very lucky indeed.

***

Sometimes his wife will approach him from behind on his weak side and playfully breath into his ringing ear in her best seductive voice, a crooked smile on her face.

"Bastard."

The word is delivered without venom in unhurried, honeyed tones, confident that there is no risk of physical retribution. Not like the good old days. He still tries to cuff her uncoordinatedly from his good side, but she is already disappearing into the kitchen, chuckling as she turns the TV up louder to drown out his grunts of protestation.

"Come and knock me about in the kitchen if you've got a problem with that, you useless lump of shit." Her words are level and considered, a deep hatred embedded in the chill of their delivery.

She slams the door, and he is left to ponder his sorry lot, the news theme playing hell with his tinnitus.

***

The following day they are blessed by a rare visit from the GP.

"You're a lucky chap," he pronounces, specs perched precariously on the end of his ruddy nose, searching hard for something positive to say. "It could have been much worse, you know?"

He pauses to take a look at the wife with a mildly salacious glint in his eye. Today in preparation for his visit she has decided to wear a tight-fitting above-knee, black skirt and full-on red lipstick.

"It looks like you're, er, being very well catered for," the GP continues, feeling somehow that the word "cater" seems more fitting than "care".

"He wants for nothing doctor. I'm here twenty-four seven for him." She smiles broadly revealing a miraculously white set of teeth.

The Sergeant splutters and tries to articulate a comment but instead descends into an uncontrollable paroxysm of coughing.

And she is there, crouching on her haunches before him, proffering a glass of water, a model of attentiveness, offering their visitor a better view of her black-stockinged thighs.

The doctor distractedly packs up his Gladstone bag and makes for a polite departure. As the front door slams, she dips her varnished fingers in the water and flicks it into his face. He farts loudly in response, wishing not for the first time, that his bowels could conjure up something more substantial.

She tweaks his cheek with a sarcastic smile.

"Ah, bless! Is that the best you can offer these days, big man?"

And she is gone, leaving behind a trail of musk that brings a tear to his good eye.

***

Being a generally unpopular figure in town, visitors to the Evans' household aren't abundant, and most of the time the Sergeant is left to his own limited devices, perched in front of the babble of daytime TV.

Constable McNabb drops by after work, and she leaves them to it without so much as the offer of a cup of tea for the visitor.

He wears his usual startled expression as his Adams Apple bobs up and down in search of words that just can't be found. He's not a man used to leading conversations.

"Nice weather."

Silence.

"The boys down the station all send their regards. Look forward to having you back."

There is a throaty noise in response that might perhaps be an ironic chuckle. It's a stupid thing to say and very in keeping with McNabb's level of intelligence.

The subjects of weather and work exhausted, McNabb is lost, and descends into an awkward silence. He starts watching the TV, commenting occasionally on the merits of the show, or the quality of the picture and sound. Eventually, defeated by the complexities of the task at hand, he rises and makes his excuses. He can't be late for the evening meeting of the snooker club committee.

"You're a lucky man, Sarge. I was worried you might not make it."

With this parting nugget of wisdom, he leaves; both parties feeling a sense of deep relief that the visit is over.

She reappears with a bowl of this evening's mushed-up food offering. "Well, that was fun, wasn't it?"

"Bisch."

***

Philip King is perplexed. In all his years at the pension department of the Police Federation, he's never come across a case stranger than this. He eyes the odd couple in question, hoping to conceal his disdain. From a financial viewpoint it would have been so much simpler if the Sergeant had just popped his clogs and gone. A simple, but generous, lump sum for the widow and it's all done. Now though, there are complex draw-down investments to consider, future care packages, mind-bending tax implications and it's his misfortune to be the one with it all cluttering up his desk.

It's now more than three weeks since the Sergeant's discharge from a lengthy stay in hospital and so far, his wife has shouldered the entire care burden. Mr King's preconception had been of a shrinking, dour, church-going type with round shoulders and a melange of cats. He is somewhat discombobulated by the brassy siren that sits attentively across from him, squeezing her husband's hand with apparently frenzied passion. A strange couple indeed. She, attractive enough in a peroxide way as his mother would have said, he, hardly God's gift. Especially now.

There were still some other irregularities that troubled him and would need to be tackled at some point. The medical report submitted to the department clearly stated that the Sergeant had suffered a stroke during the course of his duties. Yet the ambulance notes document that he was found partially clothed in the bedroom of a local woman. Constable McNabb's account of events was just an incoherent ramble. The fool seemed unable to string two sensible words together.

As a man of numbers, Mr King feels uneasy about conundrums that don't add up. His disquiet is compounded by the tantalising glimpse of the tops of Mrs Evans's stockings as she sits across from him, and the malignant, asymmetric grimace worn by her husband, breathing noisily through his nose. Still, they hold hands. He wishes she would sort out the string of dribble hanging off the poor man's chin and this train of thought leads him to the realisation that he may never truly get to the bottom of this matter.

He needs to keep things brief today.

He exchanges the standard pleasantries with all the sincerity of a man who has cut his teeth in the insurance trade. He admires Mrs Evans's new painting as he flusters over his paperwork. He is particularly complimentary about her flapjacks, inedible to the drooling husband. It is all very amicable and courteous, and any doubts that he harbours will just have to wait for another day. As he gets up to leave, he makes sure to remind them both how very fortunate the Sergeant is to have the length-of-service income protection locked into his policies and how helpful the extra money could be to them. Mrs Evans lets slip a thin smile as the Sergeant starts to snooze again.

***

"I want you to meet someone."

He is dozing gently in front of an inane game show, sleep being the preferable option, given that the TV remote has been left just out of reach.

His eyes open to see her positively radiant, broad-smiled and bouncing in front of him. It is a dull Tuesday afternoon, and she is wearing heels, tight jeans and a white blouse which is more-or-less transparent.

She steps to one side and a well-groomed man in his forties sheepishly moves into his field of vision.

"This is Clive."

The man holds up a ringless hand in greeting, looking more than a little uncertain that this introduction is appropriate.

"OK?" he says lamely.

The Sergeant sneers but can't summon himself to articulate anything coherent. He stares at the man's crotch. Wondering.

"He's from the art class and he's very kindly offered to help me sort out my easel upstairs."

The man is nodding unconvincingly, discomfited by the where the Sergeant's squinted gaze has landed.

"Yes, Catrin is very talented indeed. Lots of potential!"

There follows a silence. Clive hasn't yet grasped the Sergeant's speech limitations. Mrs Evans isn't wasting any further time. She ushers her guest back towards the hall, with the briefest wink back in the direction of her husband. The door is shut, and he hears laughter and the thump of two sets of feet rapidly ascending the stairs.

There is more bumping around overhead in what used to be the marital bedroom. Then silence. He strains hard but all he can hear is the whistling in his ears.

Time passes, it could be minutes, it could be hours. He has no idea. He is roused by the thumping descent of feet and the reappearance of Clive at the door, his hair not quite the same as it had been. He's clearly emboldened by what has passed since their previous meeting.

"Your wife is great! So talented. You're so lucky to have her."

There is a chuckle in the hallway, Mrs Evans tries to drag him out of the room.

"Anyway, it's been great meeting you Dave. I hope you get better soon"

He shuts the door with another amicable wave and is gone.

The Sergeant bristles with incandescent rage. The coup de grace has been delivered. She knows how much he hates to be called Dave.

Glaston-fucking-bury

Good, aren't they?"

The man standing beside me with the cigarette squint and the strong Welsh accent slurs at me. The "they" in question are only a few bars into their first song.

The audience in our grass-trodden amphitheatre is small, but as usual there is a hard core of ardent enthusiasts assembled at the front, already nodding like metronomes. The truth is that most of us holding tepid beers at a safe distance near the sound desk, are only here because Elton is on the other stage. Warming to me, he nudges my shoulder conspiratorially with the heel of his hand, urging some level of kinship and concordance.

Yes. They are.

I shout very loudly sipping from a cardboard cup that's about to implode. It seems a little abrupt and, not meaning to be rude in the face of a friendly salutation, I limply continue with a nod in the direction of the stage,

The guitarist is good.

He is impressed by my keen senses of observation and launches into a lengthy monologue that is largely drowned by the gut-shaking bass kicking in.

I smile back at him moronically which he clearly finds encouraging so he continues with the phrase,

"See, I'm a bit of a muso, like... "

Before once again he is submerged by thousands of decibels of warbling electronic cacophony. When I judge that he may have finished, I raise my cup to him in a gesture of benign benevolence, hoping that this will signal the conclusion of our pointless discourse, and we can both get back to the task at hand.

The music is complex, intricate, self-indulgent and

impenetrable. I won't be able to say in all honesty that I enjoyed it, but the experience is like being immersed in a deep bath of intense sensory stimuli. Lasers shimmer and arc across the clouded sky as the ubiquitous smell of dope wafts across the breeze. The group behind me light up and start a shouted and gesturing conversation in a circle, paying no attention to the what's unfolding on stage.

Staggering men who soberly scrutinise spreadsheets any other day of the year, wander around with glitter paint on their cheeks, indiscriminately snogging sozzled student nurses dressed up in bedraggled bondage gear. Bodies lie comatose on the dead grass all around us, apparently unaware that the gig has started. It's the final day of the festival and everyone and everything is looking somewhat the worse for wear.

All across the valley, lights are flashing, flags are fluttering, and strobes beam up into the darkening sky. A legion of tents surrounds us, looking down on proceedings with an air of contempt. I can catch a glimpse of the back of the crowd at the Pyramid and thank Christ I'm not in that teeming sardine can.

Behind us, at the mixing desk, the sound men stand in tight-lipped silence, giving everyone the thousand-yard stair. Their backstage passes hang nonchalantly from their necks. Look how fucking cool we are.

As if the general level of excitement isn't enough, the band announce that they have a special guest. I don't catch the name and don't recognise the diminutive figure who stumbles onto the stage in a beanie, clearly somewhat intoxicated, beaming widely at the unprecedented levels adulation from all corners of the field. My Welsh friend reaches new levels of ecstasy, and

I wonder if he may be having some sort of seizure. The guest has a droning, uncharismatic voice that I guess some love and some hate. He clearly loves it.

After a nudge-free ten minutes of noodling drivel, I cautiously turn to check on my new tactile friend. He has a crumpled cigarette flaccidly hanging from his lower lip and is bumming a light from a group of hairies the other side of him. I think I may have shaken him off before the band are moved play something I vaguely recognise, and he is up again whooping and hollering and pulling at my sleeve. Again, he nods at me for some acknowledgment, willing me to sing along with him to words that I don't know. I shake my arm up in the air rhythmically and mouth some phonetical inanities, loosely based on the sounds coming from the singer.

Inside of me there's a middle-class, white male trying to get out and ask himself, what the fuck he is doing here, and why isn't he at sitting on the sofa at home and watching the news with a nice cup of tea?

When did bands declare that the good old three-minute pop song was obsolete? Who decided that the climax of this dazzling musical extravaganza would be an elaborate pulsing light show illuminating a bored looking, inanimate bloke behind a bank of keyboards? Several checks of my watch later, the ordeal is finally over.

I turn to give him a wave or perhaps a more appropriate high-five, but he is a step ahead of me, pouncing on me and hugging me warmly, parting with a slurpy kiss on my neck. All bristles and halitosis.

I walk away wiping off the slobber of his nicotine saliva. Clearly, I have missed something in the music.

The Sergeant, Part Two

Well. You're a rare beauty, aren't you?

The Sergeant's damaged speech is slowly improving. So too is a long-forgotten, barbed sense of humour. Some would consider it unnecessarily spiteful.

The double-chinned recipient of his compliment in her starched, grey Dragon Care uniform, is unimpressed by his remarkable post-stroke progress and makes the point by making a further robust sweep of his scrotum with the rough flannel. She hates him by some margin more than she hates her own divergent squint, moley face and expansive rear end.

You're done.

Her reply is a dismissive, gruff monotone. She's endured a lifetime of jibes from arseholes like this and even though her work is lowly with piss-poor pay, she's still a million times better off than this lame duck.

He isn't finished. He tries to catch her eye with his one good one, but she steadfastly refuses to meet his crooked gaze with hers.

Still, at least you're not black, like the last one.

He sneers lopsidedly. The Sergeant is of an age to know better than to pitch crass insults, but his filter switch is well and truly burnt out. She knows an ignorant, bare-faced provocation when she hears it and will not rise to his idiotic taunts.

Princess is lovely, and you're lucky she puts up with your nonsense.

Oh, aye,

He pauses for effect,

For a dar... Ow!

Her washcloth has somehow tangled with his

catheter tube and she administers a firm yank to free it.

I could report you for that.

Now she returns his belligerent skewed glare with a grin as she bears her fag-breath down on him.

And then who would you have to do this?

Her words echo through the otherwise vacant house. Catrin's fragrance has dissipated and been replaced by the pungency of air freshener and shit. Her underwear drawer is empty, her toothbrush absent, and her handbag no longer hangs in the hallway.

She'll be back.

***

His ex-wife pouts in the bathroom mirror, a frisson of excitement that just could be nerves flutters in the centre of her abundant cleavage.

This is a big one tonight.

There had been several abortive relationship attempts since the bitter disappointment of Clive, a man who turned out to have such low levels of testosterone he could barely prop himself up. The Sergeant's hefty financial settlement had allowed her the luxuries of being able to bide her time and be more selective, but even so, there were certain limitations to living in a small Welsh town in the middle of nowhere.

So, she harbours high hopes for her latest conquest who is not only a doctor, but also five years her junior. These are significant mitigating factors for his rank halitosis, the dodgy, seventies moustache, the premature paunch and the desperate comb-over. For her part, she has changed her hair once again and is experimenting with a blonde bob for this particular romantic campaign.

The teenagers are somewhere. Maybe on sleep overs but in truth, she's not sure, nor with whom. The point is they're not going to be around tonight, and the house will be empty. The rendezvous has been agreed as a discreet dinner in a town a safe ten miles away, both acknowledging the difficulties of being easily identifiable, minor local celebrities.

She changes the sheets and tidies up the master bedroom of her rented semi. Evidence of teenaged detritus is removed from elsewhere in the house and summarily dispatched into their rooms with the doors firmly closed. In anticipation of the acceptance a nightcap, she plumps up the cushions of the sofa and rearranges the vase of flowers on the table. This attention to detail is all very well but deep down, her instincts tell her that the true measure of triumph would be a hastily procured double room at the hotel in which they will be eating.

She sprays herself with Opium one more time for luck and slips a toothbrush and a pair of knickers into her bag.

***

As a man of not unsubstantial experience with the fairer sex, he could tell from her general demeanour that it would be light work, and so it proved. But now in the cold and sober light of day, he is forced to admit that the whole thing had been something of a vanity project, and serious doubts have since intervened about the misguided wisdom of trying to get intimate with a rozzer's ex. It would cause a high-profile scandal in a town of this size and could easily draw uncomfortable questions from the wrong people about him and his past. Back in his home country, there are still plenty who'd like to sit him down for a good, long chat and set him straight on a few things.

Most of Paddy O'Hanlon's adult life had been a catalogue of questions raised, practised evasions, unworthy deeds, subtle sleights of hand, unanswered enigmas, and credibility challenges. Even now, eighteen months after his latest resettlement in Darkest Wales, he still keeps a suitcase permanently packed in his wardrobe in case of the need for rapid departure.

After a dodging and weaving history, fate has spewed him into the lauded position of a GP in this sleepy Welsh backwater, below the radar, veiled behind a bristling wall of professional respectability. Important questions that should have been asked were conveniently negotiated around. The practice, which not too long ago would never have considered employing a non-Welsh-speaking doctor, had awoken uncomfortably into a brave new world in which beggars can't be choosers. Why wouldn't they offer a post to someone of O'Hanlon's prolific experience and abilities? His CV had been impressive and clearly needed no forensic verification.

The town's inhabitants had initially displayed their usual degree of antipathy to the new arrival. The majority took a suspicious line; how could they possibly trust someone who wasn't one of their own, who didn't know their ways nor even speak their language? But, well versed in the subtleties of gaining acceptance, he played a patient game. A few strategic visits to the Bowling Club bar won over a handful of doubters, impressed by his sharp wit, apparent humility and his ability to drink ten pints of Guinness, remain standing, and be in surgery the following morning, administering reassuring Blarney bullshit.

And thus, he managed to carve out a certain reputation; his disciples and detractors citing the same evidence in the formulation of their opinion of him. In a drab town where generally speaking, there wasn't much to talk about, it didn't take long for news of him to reach her, and even less for her to concoct a chance meeting in the early disinhibited phase of one of his Bowling Club soirees, long before he was poured into a taxi and whisked the half mile home. It hadn't taken too much of her ample female guile to leave a suitable-enough impression for him to call her the following day. Like a dog with a bone.

But now they had both passed Go, the old doubts arise again in his paranoid Gaelic bones. Firstly, he has not seen her since the fateful evening of Jameson chasers, and his memory struggles to conjure up a more detailed image of her than an enticing smile and a nicely rounded figure wearing tightly fitting clothing. Her face remains something of a blur, so much so that he's not even sure if he'd recognise her if she came and seated herself right in front of him in the intimate surroundings of his own consulting room.

More importantly, there is the small matter of her estranged husband to consider. Severely disabled and housebound though he is, he still possesses a hefty reputation around town for being a mean, unpleasant bastard, and best avoided. He definitely wouldn't take kindly to the notion of O'Hanlon's Irish arse bouncing around in his wife's rented bed and could still make things very uncomfortable if he found out. These bastard rozzers all stick together. Thick as thieves.

The final undeniable consideration is his own uniquely craven disposition. A man who had swerved and weaved his way through life and never stood up for anything or anyone, least of all himself. The feigned migraine to dip out of a sticky afternoon duty, the well-rehearsed "I was never there, mate" to be deployed in a variety of situations, are worn out through overuse. It has been his natural and standard inclination to stand down from a challenge whenever one presented itself.

He chews his lip in contemplation.

**

The hotel is not how she remembered it. The mature elegance of the old coaching inn has been replaced by a beige, dog-eared shabbiness, some way short of chic. The vacant reception is bleak and unwelcoming. Off to right, the lounge is dimly lit, cold and oppressive, the furniture dark, and the curtains and cushions floral and threadbare. Even the menu, presented in sticky, dark vinyl wallets on every table, harks back several decades with prawn cocktail and soup-of-the-day featuring in the starters and black forest gateau headlining the desserts.

After an abortive scan of the bar, populated solely by a cabal of chuckling men of a certain age, she settles herself on a sofa in the adjoining lounge, near the barely lit fire to check her phone in the vain hope of a message. The barman saunters over, pursued by interested stares from the bar area. There is loud salvo of laughter from mumbled asides; it is hardly the inconspicuous, romantic atmosphere that she had hoped for. She pulls the hem of her skirt an inch or two lower, aware of the barman's gaze.

***

O'Hanlon sits himself at the tacky teak bar of the Bowling Club, transfixed by the settling head of his third pint of Guinness. His mind has worked through his extensive repertoire of excuses, and he is now more or less settled on being detained by a mortally sick child who had pitched up at the surgery at five to six. It is a risky strategy in a small town in which most genuine medical emergencies tended to leak into common knowledge within moments of them happening, but he's willing to gamble that Catrin might lack a certain appetite for gossip, given that she was very often the subject of it.

Perhaps it will be easier when the old bastard dies. If nothing else, O'Hanlon is a patient man, and he shouldn't have too long to wait if the medical records are to be relied upon.

The Guinness finally pacifies, and he takes a long, reflective sup, the froth settling like a row of icicles along his moustache. He calls the bar steward over to order a Jamesons as he dissects another beermat.

***

In the end, he had done her a favour. Whilst it has been mildly embarrassing to be the subject of so much interest and conjecture from the bar area, an intimate dinner for two, being the only couple in the place under the same level of surveillance, would have been excruciating.

142

The barman wanders over again once the locals have dispersed and exchanges a few affable words, a knowing grin hanging on his lips. His benevolence isn't lost on someone not looking her best. Knocking back a fourth vodka and lemonade, lipstick smeared and mascara tracking down her cheeks. In different circumstances she may have been asked to leave and ply her trade elsewhere.

In a not entirely altruistic act of gallantry, he offers her one of the empty guest room upstairs for less than the price of a taxi home. It's these small acts of kindness that keep her going and her skirt rides up her thighs an inch or two as she accepts with a gracious flash of her enticing smile.

The Sharpest Tool

He's not the sharpest, is he?

Mrs H invented dour. She nods disparagingly at Kyle's slouched progress across the tarmac yard below the elevated sanctity of the staff room. Harris French shakes his head, partly in disbelief, partly in apathy, as they stare out of the grubby window, the steam from the mugs of tea condensing on their spectacles. The cloying reek of his stale tobacco skirmishes with her acrid, unwashed armpits.

It's the lead in the water.

She confirms flatly with an unjustified level of authority. Harris French concurs and turns away as he reaches greedily into his jacket pocket for a Benson and Hedges.

Won't amount to much.

He mumbles as he hurries toward the fire escape, grasped by the urgency of nicotine craving. He's just glad that Mrs H doesn't smoke.

In old money, Kyle is thick as shit. No arguments.

Over their rank personal odours, tobacco fixes and milky tea, his despondent teachers have bemoaned his miserable lack of academic prowess and serially uncontrollable behaviours on a daily basis. It is widely acknowledged as a certainty that his name will never grace a GCSE certificate, and if he manages to avoid borstal, the best he could hope for is an apprenticeship in digging holes.

Unencumbered by their prejudices and his projected destiny, his hunched posture wanders menacingly around the schoolyard at break-time, wearing his aptly named donkey jacket and a threatening grimace. His

144

shovel hands clenched and twitching his pockets in the anticipation of splitting lips and blackening eyes. A box of matches rattles in his trousers, mimicking the footsteps of the imagined, like-minded army marching in his wake. He is feared, and he enjoys the accompanying notoriety.

Having no allies to speak of, apart from the handful of inadequate hangers-on who spend time with him motivated purely by self-preservation, Kyle isn't particular who he targets on any given day. The bigger the better. Although squat in build himself, he possesses the ability to effectively propel himself upwards in a corkscrew action when attempting a headbutt, catching the angle of an unguarded jaw, abruptly ending any hapless fists raised in resistance. Comical to watch, but not to be on the receiving end. He could buy a stake in the local dental surgery, the amount of work he's put their way.

He wears the obligatory black boots, laced high, scuffed, having never been graced by polish. Forensic examination might reveal blood splatters from more than one source, the thuggish badges of honour. The boots themselves are Doc Marten knockoffs acquired by his penny-pinching mother on one of her sober days from the weekly street market. No cushioned soles on these bad boys. They, like the donkey jacket, comprise his tough but thinly veneered self-identity, a clear deterrent to anyone considering a challenge to his brutal authority.

Today, Danny Edwards acts as his sycophantic partner in crime, a scrawny, piece of shit of a lad who wears a constant mean expression and a torn Harrington jacket. Together they swagger around the side of the science block intent on giving Craig Bailey the forewarned seeing-to. Threats had been issued to the lanky, ginger bastard and timings set. Now they're pumping up their adrenaline as they seek out their prey, an ominous purpose in the metre of their step. There will be detentions, or worse, but neither give much consideration to consequences. They are mindful in their violence; it's all a bit of a laugh.

Craig Bailey is waiting for them. He stands feet apart, chest inflated in defiance, facing them directly. His wingman, Crispin, carries less strut in his demeanour and is nervously holding the would-be combatant's grey duffle coat, as he swallows back the sick in his throat. He also carries with him the weight of a mother who would be very disappointed indeed to learn that he finds himself in this situation.

The plan is elegant in its simplicity. Danny will go in first with a few basic taunts along the lines of poof, wanker, ginger twat, before perhaps engaging in a little pushing and collar grappling. There may be the odd slap thrown in to encourage retaliation. This will be the signal for Kyle to swoop in defence of his comrade and start the job in earnest.

But Craig Bailey has a different and unexpected take on it all. He has tired of perpetually carrying the mantle of a lanky streak of piss and being the butt of every joke. In the privacy of his bedroom, when not masturbating, he had been putting himself through rigorous months of press-ups, pull-ups and all manner of physical challenges and tests of endurance. A Charles Atlas chest expander and a pair of dumbbells testify to the legitimacy to his regime of self-betterment. Now, beneath the weedy, unthreatening, duffle-coated

146

exterior are muscles of stone.

Emboldened by Kyle's back up, Danny kicks off with the standard, *What the fuck are YOU looking at?*

A calm folding of the arms is the response, so Danny feels compelled to stride up and give what could best be described as a half-hearted push. Craig Bailey stares him in the eye but remains taciturn and unyielding. A niggling doubt sparks in Danny's head. This is not the expected teary capitulation, but he's committed now and must press on. He screws his rat-like face into a snarl and grasps the neck of Craig Bailey's sweater, clinching it into a ball.

Think you're fucking hard do you?

Smaller kids skitter around and circle like squealing vultures. A frisson passes through the yard and some of the younger ones start the familiar *fight! fight! fight!* chant, incandescent with excitement.

But Craig Bailey is unmoved by the simmering sentiments gathering around them. He has found a deep seamed courage in his puny obscurity and covert training. There is an audible gasp followed by a stunned silence as Danny Edwards is dispatched to the ground by a single punch to the chin. Flat on his arse, he shakes his head as his tongue checks his still-reverberating teeth. Unexpected tears stream down his face and his hard-man persona evaporates in the blinking of his concussed eyes.

Craig looks as surprised as everyone else and a quorate of lice-ridden heads turn to Kyle. An inscrutable expression crosses his face as his brain tries to process the unfamiliar sensations of surprise and fear.

Go on Craig, hit him!

Crispin's knees have suddenly stopped shaking and

he finds his voice. Kyle's cogs grind slowly as he makes a mental note that perhaps the wrong target has been selected today. He finds himself stricken with indecision. The crowd is restive, feeling short changed, and yelps go up encouraging him to go over and clock him one. The adrenaline of a cornered animal flows through him and he takes a step forward.

You boys!

A familiar growl bellows down from the fire escape above them as a cigarette butt is irritably scuffed out on the steps.

Before Harris French can continue, he finds Mrs H by his side, wearing a fearsome indignation.

Kyle White, you come to my office after break time! she barks.

It is enough to disperse the labile gathering. The small ones scamper off in different directions leaving the guilty parties alone to face her wrath. Glares are exchanged but the customary parting threats are noticeably absent.

Mrs H has apparently overlooked the perpetrator of Danny Edwards's fall from grace and focussed her sizeable ire on the usual suspect. Her dressing downs are legendary and will echo across several surrounding classrooms. Harris French smiles down at her in awe and admiration. For a small, pungent woman from Burnley, she certainly knows how to clear a school yard.

Headcase

You don't need to make eye contact or speak to him to know that he's a batshit-crazy headcase.

The shimmer of perspiration on his shaven, tattooed scalp across the orange glare of the bar as he necks another shot, should be a sufficient warning of the risks those in his immediate vicinity are juggling.

Wide-eyed with arousal, he bellows slurred encouragement to those around him as more shots appear on the bar. The volume of is maniacal laugh increases as the pumping beat from the speakers notches up. He's ex-army. This isn't proper drinking. *Let's have a proper drink, eh?* He snarls.

The cuboid woman by his side shrieks in drunken mirth. She's so desperate to share her bed that she's willing to allow the alcohol to jaundice her better judgment, a decision that her bruised body will regret in the morning.

The dangerous hour before closing time is approaching and those sober enough with any remaining sense, edge gently away from him, towards quieter, darker tables in dimly lit corners. They've seen it all before a hundred times; an explosion of violence is only a hair-trigger away.

In the lounge bar next door, an unknowing stranger, quietly sups his Guinness, glued to his mobile, keeping himself to himself, unaware of the dire peril a simple trip to empty his bladder presents.

There will be a meeting over the urinals, one slumped with his forehead against the tiled wall, powder in his nostrils, pissing on his shoes, while the other flounders ineffectually with the buttons of his flies.

An unintentional brush while passing towards the sinks will lead to an apology, followed by a wild swing and a resounding crack. One will end up having plastic surgery, County Durham-style.

The Sergeant, Part Three

Since she left, the diaphanous divide between life and death has been stretching precariously thin for the Sergeant. It wasn't that she had contributed even the smallest grain of positivity to his overall quality of life over these past few difficult months, but the acerbic nature of her presence had at least provided him with a mild frisson in an otherwise colourless existence. Now, in his fusty solitude, he feels even more worthless and discarded.

Whereas some are lucky enough to recover completely from a stroke, the Sergeant has been less favoured. After the initial optimism of the first few weeks when he made impressive progress, fine-tuning the abuse of his carers and becoming more like his old, scathing self, his demeanour gradually changed, and his health embarked on a steadily downward spiral. It soon became clear that the meandering pathway to his demise was more a question of when than if.

In her absence, the trajectory of his decline had been alarming to anyone showing the merest, passing interest in his wellbeing. But his friendship group, which had been fragile and select at the best of times, vanished completely subsequent to the unfortunate event and he was left with a revolving door of clock-watching carers, more interested in scribbling inanities in their notes rather than his general welfare.

Constable McNabb's early efforts in offering support, more out of a sense of duty than any true camaraderie or respect, had become too much of a burden for him, and rumour had it that he now spent most weekday evenings sitting in miserable, silent solitude at the bar of the Bowling Club, drinking alcopops and staring at the optics.

The kids are the worst. Teenaged, disinterested, loaded with hormones and surly in their black attire and assorted perforations. There's never been any love lost and it's clear that their visits now are always under duress. They clump in with all the sensitivity of bulldozers, either yawning, giggling or eating crisps.

Alright Dad?

By rote, like they're expecting a response. His sideways glare is bereft of paternal warmth. He wishes they'd just fuck off. He's not even sure if they're his.

Sometimes, when they don't get the message, he closes his eyes and feigns sleep. Apart from encouraging a precipitous departure, it also enables him to listen to them talk more freely. More often than not, they just come so that they can openly smoke without fear of a telling off. The place stinks anyway so no one is in the least perturbed by a whiff of stale fag smoke hanging in the air. They speak in something less than reverent tones.

He looks shafted. How long do you think the fucker's going to carry on for?

A snigger.

Maybe he needs a little help?

A pillow is poised mid-air above his head, half in jest.

I didn't know that vegetables dribble and smell of shit.

He farts loudly to clear them out in a tittering, gagging retreat.

His previous propensity to eating almost anything put in front of him has depleted into a pathetic dependence on others to ensure that food reaches his mouth from the plate. His premorbid limited powers of communication have withered into grunts of one-syllable. His asymmetric facial grimace seems to have further tightened and contorted. Now, most days are spent in an inanimate drowse, slack-jawed, saliva running down his chin, lying low under a blanket of interminable boredom.

Alright Dave?

The care team attends to hoist him out of bed and manhandle his twisted form into a position resembling comfort in the wipe-clean vinyl chair, bolstered to an impossible angle by an army of pillows and cushions. Each morning, they leave him dangling in mid-air to check his wizened arse for signs of broken skin and to whip around his sorry genitalia with a wet flannel. His gurgles of protest are usually met with light-hearted fripperies, tainted with the occasional harsh edge, but invariably ignored. He waits until they've finished and padded him up before unloading his bowels, replenishing the house with its ubiquitous stench.

The TV is switched on and they go about their business with the irritating, chirrup of the morning news in the background. A breakfast of lukewarm porridge and mashed up banana is prepared and spooned into his unappreciative, sneering gob. The bits he manages to spit back are caught in the spoon and recycled straight back in. *Come on now Dave, stop fucking about. Eat up.*

The fucking slag, as he'd like to call her if he still were blessed with the ability to do so, is nowhere to be seen these days. There was no sad adieu, no words even, just a minicab driver carrying off her stuff into his seven-seater and an echoing final slam of the front door. He doesn't know where she's gone. No one volunteers the information, and he no longer holds the capacity to ask the question.

Incandescent. He could swing for every single fucking one of them. His livid anger is the only thing that keeps his blood pumping.

But even that is finite and as the weeks drag on, a dull monotony intervenes, and apathy replaces the fading anger. It doesn't take much to knock him over, the dying light of autumn and an epidemic. His morning carers arrive laughing and joking and, stubbing out their cigarettes, find him limp and lifeless in a puddle of his parting gift. His previously contorted face now symmetrical and peaceful. A life of feisty contrariness ends in a lonely, inauspicious, shit-smelling capitulation.

***

Later, that same day, after they have cleaned him up and carted him and all his medical paraphernalia away, she comes around to pay her respects to the empty house. She wears a pair of fake Wayfarers, red lipstick, gun-metal nails, a low-cut red top and tight, white jeans. The only widow's black in evidence is the lacey strap of her bra.

She has requested to be left in respectful peace and solitude. A time for pensive reflection and an undisturbed opportunity to rustle through the drawers in search of anything of value the carers may have missed. She routes out a few bits of silver tittle tattle that are hastily loaded into a Tesco bag. At the back of the sideboard, she finds their dusty wedding album.

Back in those days, it was customary not to smile for

wedding photographs but to pose in a forced, stiff formality for the camera. Get it over with. Much like the wedding night for her. She stares at the two grim, much younger faces and wishes she could turn back the clock and tell her younger self to not be such a fool. The notion that marrying a policeman carried any weight of respectability was ridiculous, even then. What a miserable waste the last twenty years had been for both of them.

She had been relieved when he grew frustrated by her repeated defiance in the face of his demanding sexual proclivities and took his physical needs elsewhere. On the mantelpiece there remains a large tub of Vaseline which they had latterly been using to rub on his chapped lips. She laughs.

She sits at the table which in the non-too-distant past hosted many a hostile family meal and stares out of the window at the grey clouds swirling rapidly to the east. Their movement prompts a heightened sense of time passing and unexpected tears of well up. Lost youth, lost time, a lost life. A confluence of grief overwhelms her in this dingy, stinking epitaph to a miserable past.

The temptation is to blame him for it all but, even though her levels of hatred for the man are no less acute for his passing, she knows the culpability is shared. We're all responsible for our own happiness, as Clive had once expounded in an uncharacteristic turn of eloquence, whilst zipping himself up in a rush to leave. Wisdom was not something she had generally credited him with during their brief dalliance, but he was bang on with that one, dickhead though he remains.

She loses herself in a fog of what-might-have-beens.
Alright Dave?

Dr O'Hanlon lets himself in through the back door and removes his flat cap. He laboriously sucks on a Tic-tac, hung over, and clearly a page or two behind the rest of the world. Had he bothered reading through his morning's emails rather than hiding in the toilet for forty-five minutes doing the crossword, he would have been aware of the Sergeant's departure and his scheduled palliative care visit could have been more productively spent. Unless of course his actions had been slyly contrived in the expectation of finding her there. He raises his eyebrows and looks surprised, a master of false sincerity.

Catrin, I didn't expect... where's Dave?

He is a little too casual, a smidgen too flippant. But there again, that is his way.

He's gone. Not before time.

She wipes away the tears from her cheeks, realising their incongruity with her last remark.

I'm so sorry...

Don't be. I think you probably know how it was. Good riddance...

Yes, of course, I'm sorry though, I didn't know. To be sure.

She is silent, letting this probable lie float in the fetid, serendipitous air. There is an awkward pause, each waiting for the other to bring up a certain subject. O'Hanlon, with uncharacteristic courage, breaks the silence.

Well now then, I'll best be off. I don't want to be disturbing you.

She notices how he leans heavily on his Irish vernacular in a hollow effort to convince her of his veracity. She's about to tell him to fuck off, doctor or no

156

doctor. But then he pauses at the door before delivering a line of such plausible grace, it has to be sincere.

Actually Catrin, I think I owe you an apology.

Oh yes? How's that then?

She purses her lips and gestures that he should take the seat on the sofa facing her.

He clocks the lipstick, the gun metal nails and the bra strap and for the briefest and rarest of moment, Paddy O'Hanlon is left without words. He wishes he still had a Tic-tac in his parched mouth. He sits down and lays the Nike rucksack, in which he keeps his clinical equipment, on the table.

The night that we were supposed to meet. You know?

He nods in her direction to urge her to remember the unforgettably awful trauma of being left hanging in a hotel bar barely a month before. The earth could have swallowed her up with shame and embarrassment. She can still taste the barman's nicotine tongue and feel his fumbled gropings on her cringing skin.

The one when you didn't turn up. Yes, I remember.

Well, I meant to come, of course, but that afternoon I found out that one of my old pals back home, you know. Died. And I was stuck on the phone to his poor mammy for hours. I was so upset that I just forgot about the rest of the world. Like.

It's a long reach even for O'Hanlon's well-honed audacity. She is well used to the smell of bullshit but part of her really wants to believe him. It's the same part that wants to believe every man she meets. There are a few moments silence while she weighs up the pros and cons of absolution.

Why don't we at least let him go cold, Paddy?

He takes her use of his Christian name as a hint of reconciliation and under the circumstances, realises that it's the best that he can hope for.

You know, Catrin, it's customary in my profession to follow up a death with a phone call to the bereaved, just to check up they're okay, like...

He pauses as he ponders if he may be overstepping the mark,

Perhaps...?

He takes her hand across the table in his own sweaty palms in a clumsy expression of empathy.

She'd like to say that she doesn't know about him. Like the many others in the town that share the same emotion, a deep uncertainty about Dr O'Hanlon. But that wouldn't be true; she is an expert on men like him. She can see through his superficial falseness and read his sordid intentions as if he were flying them from a flagpole.

Catrin shakes her head, as if trying to suppress an internal argument. She stands up, picks up O'Hanlon's bag from the table and pushes it into his paunch. She walks to the door, opens it and stands to one side, indicating that his visit is over.

He nods and pulls up his ill-fitting Chinos as he stands. There is a faint smell of Tic-tacs as he wafts past the threshold without a word. She is touched by the sorrowful figure he cuts as he slouches down the path towards his car, and she can't help but call after him that he still has her number before shutting the door.

Blue Lines

Sarah holds the little white stick in front of her like a talisman, gently pincered between her carefully manicured nails. She can't bear to open her eyes to receive the message it delivers. She has come this far, through all of their detestable procedures. Counselled, poked, prodded, scanned, inseminated and now the simple act of parting her eyelids is just too much.

Her bare buttocks shiver against the cold plastic of the toilet seat. There, in the insipid morning light, talcum powder motes dance. She can still smell his aftershave.

She would be fine. She is strong, a thoroughbred from sturdy Anglo-Saxon stock. A fine pedigree with generations of emotional desensitising. A glimpse at her Facebook page would tell you that she is the real deal. It's Felix that worries her.

Not a man to accept his shortcomings lightly, it had been a testing enough task to persuade him to engage with whole IVF bandwagon in the first place. His pride had been wounded by the ignominy of his test results. Few knew, only one or two carefully selected, discreet friends. Although they had shared their difficulties with her parents, there was no way that Felix's pride would allow anything to slip in front of his. It was as if he thought they didn't already know.

Then there was his enforced gardening leave. The police force can be an unforgiving organisation to those perceived to have transgressed. There are always two sides to every story although this basic truth is rarely acknowledged by the media. He had been apparently lucky to have kept his job. Employed, but tarnished goods.

As usual, the gin had taken a hit, and an unrecognisably subdued man had replaced the previously ebullient ray of light she had married. How she so yearned that all his quips of getting in some practice on their honeymoon had borne the wished-for fruit.

Her mind wandered back to their wedding day. His dad's speech had been replete with pride and emotion leaving the room sniffing and pensive. Mascara ran in streams, and she had been shocked to see Felix in tears; now she barely sees him without tell-tale red eyes.

The eternal optimist, she had projected the IVF as a beacon of hope, never once considering that after two failed attempts, the effect would be quite the opposite. Three times lucky she had insisted.

AND TODAY WAS THE DAY.

He knew that well enough but had still been quick to excuse himself this morning. A much longer run than usual. Perhaps there was more to this new health kick than meets the eye.

She had always been able to scratch below the surface and seen the depth and sensitivity behind the pumped-up chest and throwaway one-liners. After the initial attraction of his wickedly sharp sense of humour, it had been this recognition that had cemented their relationship.

Everyone agreed they were great together. What a brilliant family they would be. They hadn't deserved all of this.

So, where was he?

***

Adie enjoys watching Sarah. His past observations had always been surreptitious, covert even. Peering through the tangle of the yew hedge whilst performing essentials of garden maintenance, pristine shears in hand. A perfunctory glance in her direction as she hung out the washing while he manoeuvred his lawn mower in seated, and apparently blissful, concentration. His elegant parallel lines were the source of much personal pride and solace.

Ah yes, her washing. It's not Felix's running gear that draws his interest.

His business partner's insistence that he now must work from home three days a week has opened up all sorts of tantalising new opportunities. Jem had been quick to nominate him for what remained of the school runs allowing her to suffer her migraines in the undisturbed, curtained, solitude of their marital bed.

His extended chores offered him the exciting discovery that by standing in a particular spot in Ivan's bedroom, he had an angled, although unobscured view of the en-suite next door. A glimpse of a bare shoulder whilst he waited for furred milk teeth to be cleaned properly had been his only rewards so far. But the possibilities were delicious.

There are binoculars on the wish list of his Amazon account, and he has already begun sowing the seeds of a ruse by professing a keen interest in the local owl population. It wasn't that Jem took much notice of his interests these days but his is a character of careful risk-assessment and considered contingencies. It was around this time that he had also recently noted the pressing need for shelving in Ivan's room. Not a man to do things in half measures, he would obviously need to give this matter his prolonged and diligent attention.

This morning, he finds himself rearranging Ivan's t-shirts again; this time in colour-order. As neatly stacked as he had left them yesterday. The previous pre-teen-aged mayhem of the room had started to show signs of order, courtesy of his fastidious attentions. Fine tuning, a paternal guiding light.

Jem has ventured away from the sterile sanctity of their bedroom on the premise of a socially distanced coffee with a coven of school mum friends. There is peace in the house, so Ivan and Amy presumably sit glued to a screen, in thumb-sucking bliss and he is alone in his thoughts, staring lasciviously at the top of her raven bob, apparently seated in lengthy contemplation.

An oppressive feeling of pining loneliness descends upon him here in the dusty muddle of a four-year-old's bedroom. It is not entirely alien, this cloying pang of regret steeped in heady nostalgia. The banished, needling, bitterness of loss, the ghostly urge of forgotten and forbidden fruit. The waft of hormones not yet entirely exhausted.

No good could come of resurrecting the past. He recognises a profound longing that goes far beyond an unhealthy eyebrow raise to his neighbour. There is a growing sense that on reaching the highly respectable milestone of forty-eight years, maybe the world isn't the oyster that it had once seemed.

Accountancy had been kind. A gleaming, over-washed, Lexus is parked like a trophy on his impeccable driveway. A quietly elegant, detached house sits behind with an immaculately tended lawn. A comfortably black bank balance allows extravagant family holidays and a new patio. A depressed wife whom he can't remember the taste of. And kids he struggles to connect with, even during the enforced shared space of lockdown.

That was more-or-less the sum of things.

A thud followed by an indignant yell disturbs his luxuriant vigil and signals an incipient riot downstairs. He leaves Ivan's door open, anticipating a return visit later on, but for the time being he scurries down the perfectly vacuumed stairs feeling short-changed.

***

The disappointment weighs heavily on her shoulders as she trudges back up the hill. It had been a thoroughly unfulfilling and unsatisfactory afternoon. The coffee had tasted insipid and lukewarm from her ineffectual Telly Tubbies flask and gossip just didn't work behind masks; the subtleties were lost. When asked, she had alluded with a courageous resignation to the less-than-ideal circumstances at home. As usual, her kids were the unwarranted victims of her criticism. She had pronounced with an unchallenged level of certainty that Ivan suffers from ADHD. Few members of the gathering volunteered anything positive about having their respective partners at home during normal working hours. Just more work and no help with anything. Hopeless. Why had it taken a lockdown for them to all realise?

The levity of the gathering had not presented the opportunity to broach the subject of her loneliness. There was a risk in breaking cover, drawing attention to the carefully camouflaged fragilities of her home life. It was silly anyway; how could anyone possibly feel alone in a house in which personal space is at such a premium?

163

From the tone of conversation around her it seemed that her dreary circumstances were widely shared.

It is therefore in a somewhat sombre, reflective frame of mind that she spots Felix, resplendent in his ubiquitous Lycra sitting on the bench overlooking the brown fields. His gaze is in the opposite direction of her approach so she could easily walk behind him, and he would be none-the-wiser. But that wasn't Jem's nature and right now any social contact outside her home is preferable to the alternative.

***

The truth was that he had felt ambushed, violated even, by her cloddish intrusion. Even one of her awful kids could have interpreted his posture as warning "do not disturb".

Most of the last hour had been spent in silent, seated contemplation, staring at nothing in particular. A million thoughts came and went, all emanating from the same central theme.

"Hiya!"

Jem had beamed from a suitably safe social distance and waved at him unnecessarily.

He had wiped his face on the pretence of sweating and smiled, disguising his annoyance, whilst feeling partially relieved to be diverted from increasingly distressing thought processes. They embarked on their usual convivial but inconsequential conversation. You look well, a compliment exchanged in full complicit knowledge that they both looked terrible. Jem was stick thin as ever, her dry stringy hair hanging limply around her pale, wanness. Yes, Sarah's great; Adie, yes, he's good too, enjoying some quality time at home with the kids, still keeping really busy. Her migraines had been troublesome and meant that she's had to spend much of the past two weeks in bed. Yes, good to get out, etc. They parted agreeing that it was a shame that The White Hart had fallen victim to the hard times and the promise of getting together sometime soon for a tea and chinwag over the fence when the weather obliges.

Now as Felix stands on his front path and stares up, he can see that the light is still on in the en-suite above the front door. He cannot remember a time when he has felt worse. She's been in there for ages, since he'd left. That surely can mean only one thing. His heart races and perspiration breaks out on his brow. There is a rhythmic throbbing in his temple.

He is too scared to believe any other outcome than yet another failure. He was a bad loser in the best of times and in the past had been prone to petulant tantrums when sporting jousts had not gone his way. Now, almost every day feels like just another capitulation. How desperately he needs something to go right for a change. He chokes up again as his thoughts once again painfully meander back to the way they had all treated him, the feeling of rejection, the rebuke, the written warning and now the freezing out. He knows there is no way back.

He is scared out of his wits that he will lose Sarah too. It doesn't take a genius to work out that she's still young enough to start again with a better-functioning member of his gender and she still turned heads when they used to go out socialising. But beautiful though she remains, he can see that some of her previous effervescent lustre has depleted in recent months, and

165

you can only blame lockdown and hormone treatments so far.

Being ambushed by Jem and her interminable desire to exchange tittle-tattle had been unwelcome but nevertheless pleasantly distracting as it turned out. But he can't postpone the inevitable any longer. He puts on a swagger of quiet optimism as he begins walking up the path, in case she might be monitoring his progress through the slatted bathroom blinds. As he puts his key in the lock, he hears a cry from the bathroom above. He drops his keys in panic on the steps up to the door. He squats to pick them up and in doing so notices the pink-shirted man in the window of the house opposite, drawing the curtains.

They wave unconvincingly.

Yesterday's Cereal

Once again it was the rain that woke him. Drumming relentlessly on the peeling sash window. The swish and sway of passing traffic. Oaths muttered by people splashing their ways down the pavement outside. Standard Welsh weather.

His pasty lids, mired together like ancient grey envelopes, flicker ineffectively in the effort of opening. A groan. A bad smell emanating from under the duvet. A sandpaper tongue lolling in the blighted desert of his mouth. The toxic fumes of his breath shroud pregnantly over his crumpled pillow. A bloodshot eye heaves open to survey the opprobrium; the dreary, insipid quality of the autumnal light making any estimation of time an impossibility.

His bedside table reflects the general chaos of his life. Yesterday's cereal bowl with cornflakes cemented to the side like crustaceans over a pool of curdled milk. Surrounding it are various items of detritus; discarded balls of tissue paper, a crushed, half empty can of Red Stripe and a limp pack of Marlboros, gaping in its desolation. Empty condom wrappers lie haphazardly on the bedroom floor; the general sense of Eighties paranoia prohibiting intimate contact via any other means.

The door to the living room stands boldly ajar, telling tales on the miscreant living room beyond. Dust ghosts dance in the thin light and Dreggs can hear the pecking staccato of some blithering BBC tosser gobbing off about picket lines and government policy and other stuff that doesn't, and will never, interest him. The TV, a lonely sentinel guarding the bleakness of his dilapidation through night and day.

His head pounds in time with the erratic rhythm of the rain, ears still ringing in a high pitch whistle from the gig last night. Movement would result in vomiting; of that he is certain. Much safer to stay beneath the barricade of bedding.

He smears a sticky hand across his face and sniffs loudly. Her scent still hangs oppressively in the air and on his skin, but Mara has gone. Her side of the bed ruined but vacant. Wary of stirring the evil spirits lurking within him, he rotates, slowly and deliberately to face her perfect impression in the mattress. Wild, untameable Mara. What a catch she had been. What a surprise that she had chosen him in the first place. Big, ugly, goofy, cloddish, oafish, thick-as-shit Dreggs. Familiarities that he had become accustomed to over the years.

The courtship had been brief, he had likened it to winning the Lottery without having bought a ticket. Hunched over a coffee in the cafe waiting for Jonny Mac to turn up with some dope, she had sat herself opposite, a welcome but uninvited surprise. His opinion was not sought; she had simply assumed that he would accept and acquiesce. And he did. Without so much as a second thought.

She had turned up at his flat only a few hours later with a rucksack slung over her shoulder. It was unceremoniously discarded on the kitchen floor while they sealed the contract on his sofa and there she had remained; four months; until this morning.

His Clash poster hangs limply from the wall, Paul Simonon posturing as though midway through a forward somersault over his fragmenting bass. A blood stained Relax t-shirt lies screwed up and discarded on the end of the bed. Not hers, for she only ever wears black. The doors of the cheap pine wardrobe at the end of the bed hang open; broken in the semblance of a corpse on a gibbet, his and her clothes spewing out of it and strewn like entrails across the threadbare carpet.

His prominent brow furrows further in weight of concentration, trying to gather his whirling and confused thoughts. There had been a row, that much he remembers, and it had been a slow burner, brewing for most of the previous day. The details of the events of the evening remain blurred, a fog of alcohol, dope and Es, but with a considerable effort of will, he rewinds further back to the late morning when the sparring had started.

Clearly, the ring idea had backfired. Stupid, stupid, stupid. He speaks these words out loud, and they reverberate through the emptiness, unanswered.

Why had he done it? He wasn't even sure himself. It all seems so patently ridiculous in retrospect. It was him all over.

Not a man who easily expresses his emotions, the intention had been to demonstrate his commitment to her, be it in a fumbled and awkward manner. There had also been a hefty helping of tongue-in-cheek, with more than a passing reference to her eccentric dress sense and clunky jewellery.

For the ring itself had been a monstrosity, impressive only in its proportions. It had been deliberately rubbed and tarnished to make it look worn and faux antique. Stupid runes and stars and stuff were etched into it like the cover of the Led Zep album he had once owned but traded for a sixteenth of black. He had found it at the bottom of a stale smelling cardboard box whilst unloading stuff down at Ned's junkshop. It had been full of the usual porcelain trinkets and other old people's crap but as soon as he saw the ring, he thought of her. Ned had simply shrugged to his gruff plea for ownership, drew on his rollie and returned to his sci-fi paperback with an apathetic fart.

Feeling like an exuberant kid again, he had presented the ring to her after breakfast. There had been no ceremony; he wasn't a man for that kind of thing, but she had nevertheless reacted as he had hoped, greedily dragged it onto her right thumb after it proved too big for any of her fingers. She smeared her dark purple lipstick noisily across his lips and quipped hoarsely, "You always did remind me of Gollum."

The reference had been lost on him as was any semblance of a retort. He stood with a mute frown, considering the possibility that her remark may have been a compliment while she turned away, headphones in her ears, singing absent-mindedly. A change had come over her; she had been strangely cold and detached, not the same woman with whom he had awoken that morning in a passionate clinch.

They didn't talk much on their way to the Red. Her characteristic lop-sided grin was in little evidence. She must have liked the ring though, the way she surreptitiously fondled it in her jacket pocket. Normally she would have babbled on inanely about anything and everything, an incorrigible tsunami of words, but that evening she had been strangely subdued and silent. Hormones, perhaps.

The dank October air and squally rain had made him more tight-lipped and uncommunicative than usual as he brooded miserably, wishing he were more her equal. In the time they had spent together, the feeling of him always being two steps behind whatever she was thinking had been inescapable. His affection for her should have made him feel better than it did.

Striding on through the murk, they eventually reached the rowdy camaraderie of the Red, with its strong lager, cheap narcotics and cacophonous music, proven antidotes to the deepest of depressions. Rhythm Method were playing in the back room and the place was heaving.

His head starts to pound again in the effort of recall. It had been a pretty good night until returning from the bar, he spotted her dancing with Kyle. The two of them had seemed just a little too unaware of everyone else around them, especially the big, gangly guy with the prominent forehead, awkwardly holding two drinks. They had embraced. Had he seen her hand rummaging in Kyle's pocket? Hadn't he returned to the safety of the bar to prop it up disconsolately with glass of JD in front of him? Hadn't he searched for her after the band had finished, finding her in the back yard with smeared make up and dishevelled hair? Pogoing at the front, she'd said. And hadn't Kyle conspicuously disappeared before the end?

They had rowed openly in the pub, sulked and sniped on the way home, both verbally abusing the drunken hulk of Fat Barnes slumped and incoherent in a pool of his own body fluids outside the Chinese. Escalating, hair had been pulled, oaths shrieked, and blows landed.

He feels a sudden pain in his left cheek as he recalls her alarming violence with a further rush of nausea. Unsteadily, he lurches out of bed and propels himself towards the toilet, reaching it just in time, his body exploding into paroxysms of vomiting. Throwing himself against the porcelain he retches uncontrollably for what seems like an eternity before sprawling spent against the side of the sink, the orange linoleum floor oscillating and vertiginous in front of him.

Breathing heavily, he draws himself up to a standing position and rests his head against the mirror, surveying the grizzly reflection. Red eyes, grey skin, sunken cheeks and cracked lips, no different to any other morning after a night at the Red. At the centre of the swollen bruise adorning his left cheek is a cut in the perfect shape of a star where the ring had branded itself on him.

Something to remember her by.

Costa Fucking Rica

Through practised stealth, the bugger's managed to nonchalantly slip it into conversation once again.

Somewhere across the Zoom ether, I hear a despairing groan from a like-minded microphone that hasn't been muted.

He's been there in the past, on some kind of cultural exchange of smug dickheads, travelling gratis under the flimsy camouflage of academia. Unfortunately for the rest of us, he wasn't suitably enamoured with the place to extend his visit into something more permanent. Either that, or they spotted a prize bore, even across the language barrier, and dispatched him sharpish.

He enjoys sharing his exquisite Costa Rican insights whenever he can, it somehow elevates him to a higher station than us lesser mortals, unfamiliar with the unique metre of its regional poetry.

He is hoping that someone, unacquainted with his historical tedium, will feel moved to invite him to read some of his own poetry, inspired by its mystic exoticism, but mercifully the Zoom meeting falls into an awkward, stubborn silence.

As a man who enjoys the sound of his own voice and the sharing of his brilliantly perceptive cerebrations, he continues undaunted for another minute or two, before offering to play us a traditional folk song on his ocarina. I sense a ripple of collective panic across our Internet enclave, and I'm relieved when the Chair intervenes with an embarrassed cough and a stutter of thanks, reminding us that we're behind schedule.

We are temporarily reprieved but I know it won't be long before his virtual hand will be up again offering a sensitive and considered Costa Rican perspective. On the chat, one of the Birkenhead clowns suggests that maybe we could all bring along our favourite Central American musical instrument to the next meeting.

One thing I'll miss about Zoom when we eventually return to more traditional meetings of the face-to-face variety: the off switch.

The Wild West

There's a palpable poverty here. It permeates through the skin and chokes innards like a cancer.

She surveys the rough piece of scrubland where kids come to play football and fight. Blood has been spilled on the feeble grass where the dog now hunkers down and empties its bowels. She considers leaving the steaming pile where it is. Surely no one here will care either way.

This place, where many a happy hour had been spent in the innocence of childhood, is now just intrinsically sad. The view of the majestic, shallow valley through which the River Vyrnwy meanders below has been hijacked by the dourness of the square, red-bricked council houses that lie only a poo-bag's throw away from her. Bent and rusting mesh fences divide overgrown back gardens, littered with discarded white goods, broken toys and incessantly barking dogs.

It has clearly been an error of judgement to come up here. The anticipated uplift from rose-tinted nostalgia has been usurped by the general decay of the years passing. A scene that was once familiar and calming is now simply bleak.

She turns away, whistles the dog and walks on up the brackened hill past discarded tyres and the carcasses of a couple of mattresses. The flecks of slate on the path allow her boots enough purchase to counteract the slickness of the mud as sheep skitter and shit in front of her. She reaches the top with a sweat on her back and breathless but without undue embarrassment.

She is relieved that everything does indeed look better with the benefit of distance. A neon-infused haze hangs over the town beyond the estate. Bustling isn't the word, but a community full of beating hearts, nonetheless.

She pulls out a pack of cigarettes from her coat pocket, experiencing a fleeting, but familiar, feeling of guilt as she flicks open the lid. Old habits die hard. She taps the tip of her cigarette on the box before lighting. A ritualistic gesture that serves no purpose that she can see. A bit like living in this place.

If the environs are anything to go by, at some point in time, it must have been beautiful here. She can't imagine the level of post-war desperation that led to the construction of places like the Brownhill Estate. Economic constraints aside, it was the sheer, dull-minded, short-sighted, lack of imagination that riled her most. This brick-and-mortar misery was man-made. There was no force of nature to blame here.

Even in the nascent shine of the Twenty-First Century, this place feels like a frontier town, replete with feckless blow-ins, bedraggled no-hopers and stubborn, stoical aboriginals with lower lips perpetually indented with teeth marks. There is a sense of impatient anticipation here. No frisson of excitement, just waiting for something to happen to break the self-imposed monotony and challenge generation upon generation of the stagnant status quo.

A few years ago, during one of her flying summer holiday visits, some kids had set fire to the top of the hill overlooking the town sparking a wave of righteous indignation extending as far as the proposition from some of the more vocal residents that conscription should be restored. Last year, one enlightened soul had graffitied an ejaculating penis on a prominent rock face on the same hill, provoking a more muted public

176

reaction. It was painted over within a week.

The grey drabness of the town nestles within the understated grandeur of breath-taking mountains, like a festering pustule on the snow-white skin of an infant. It connects to the rest of civilisation through twenty miles of winding, sometimes vertiginous roads to the north, south and east. A few miles westward walk along the boggy banks of the river and the salty tang of the lurking Irish Sea fills your lungs.

Even having travelled widely, the Vyrnwy Estuary ranks highly as one of the most beautiful places that she has ever seen, espccially viewed from one of the wild, windy overlooking ridges on a fine spring day. Those very peaks make up the rolling skyline visible from her current vantage point, turning purple in the last vestiges of sunlight from what had been a fine October day. She exhales the cigarette smoke pensively from her nostrils and wishes she could teleport herself. Some talked of the untamed country surrounding the town as being the closest resemblance to true wilderness south of Scotland. She couldn't disagree. But wild places breed wild people, rough-edged and un-nuanced.

She takes a long, greedy drag before flicking the cigarette away onto the muddy path she has just climbed. There is no escaping the deep ambivalence she feels here. It's almost as if the uneasy relationship between the conurbation and the country surrounding it reflects her own relationship with the town's natives. For, disregarding the chaotic eyesore of the estate below her, she could easily be tempted to return here if it wasn't for the people.

Constipated in every sense and hopelessly blinkered, they had always struggled to accept that one of their own, especially a female no less, could grow wings and make a success for herself in the outside world without so much as a hike-up marriage to a bank manager. Why couldn't she have just hitched up with a farmer or worked in a shop like the rest?

She had left this place so full of promise and optimism. It had been like a weight lifting, the world outside offering an overdue refuge from this oppressive atmosphere. A place where you were sneered at for revealing a nugget of intelligence or a modicum of imagination. A place where you were bullied because you didn't speak the language or belonged to a family that owned two cars. A hard, uncompromising and insignificant spot on the map with a population united in belligerent jealousy of everything beyond their blinkered world and a deep-rooted communal sense of injustice and subjugation.

There is suddenly a chill in the air that causes a shiver down her spine. The acrid waft of coal smoke drifts up to her hill and hits the back of her throat. She is glad to have had the foresight to bring his old cardigan.

Turning out the old house had been one of the most painful experiences of her life and judging by the sheer volume of tittle-tattle rubbish that her mother had accumulated over her many years of widowhood, she judged that she had not much else to look forward to for the next week at least. But amongst the dusty tears there had been small triumphs.

She sniffs the sleeve; it still smells of his pipe tobacco even after all these years. She could picture him sitting in his armchair after work doing the crossword, glasses perched halfway down his nose, half-watching the TV. He had not wanted to raise a family here. He would have preferred to have stayed in Manchester after his university education but had succumbed to pressure from his overbearing family to return to the country of his birth. Her mother never fully forgave him for being dragged, pregnant and unwilling, to this "arse-end of a place" as she had so eloquently, repeated in her lilting Liverpudlian vernacular. She had never been accepted and took it hard, the animosity mutual.

The exploring dog starts barking as two hooded youths appear over the brow of the hill on bikes that look a couple of sizes too small for them. Their faces are dimly illuminated by glowing cigarettes. They don't notice her perched on a rock beside the path. They are chatting, spitting and swearing in English, uncouth harsh syllables, hard vowels and profanities. They pass by close enough for her to smell the chip fat and burnt heroin off their unwashed bodies before descending down the hill laughing, their bony arses tipping out of tracksuit bottoms more proportioned to the bikes than the wearers.

She tracks them down the hill, malevolence permeating from their diminishing forms, the glowering sentinels patrolling the periphery of their domain. She is well used to native hostility.

Earlier in the day she had needed relief from the dusty mayhem of house clearing. Feeling emotionally and physically drained, she locked up and made her way down the High Street with a faint stir of optimism in her heart. She had been away sufficiently long to escape the hindrance of recognition, although part of her still longed to bump into one of the old crowd.

Change can be shocking. The once proud family businesses had more or less capitulated, leaving in their wake a mushrooming influx of hairdressers, pound shops and charity stores. A Polish delicatessen had materialised for no apparent rhyme or reason where the old shoe shop used to be. A Vape shop had replaced the newsagents where she had accompanied her father as a child to buy the Sunday newspaper. The takeaways and pubs seemed to be the only places in town doing any sort of decent business.

She stepped over a pool of vomit by the bus stop. Inane graffiti speckled the red Perspex. Tomos is a prick. Kerry4Clive. Man U twats. A hastily scribbled reproduction of the ejaculating penis. On the bench, a half-drunk bottle of Coke resided beside strewn crisp packets. The discarded debris of youth burdened by boredom.

As she moved toward the heart of the town the pavements busied with what seemed like the detritus of humanity. Middle aged, ruddy men carrying their paunches with a certain, indignant pride, ignorantly awaiting the arrival of their first stroke. Pudgy, mothers in scruffy black hoodies and ill-fitting sweatpants texting disinterestedly while pushing buggies loaded with bawling, feral toddlers.

It was no surprise to find the Market Hall at the epicentre of adolescent angst. Groups of youths slouching and scowling around the entrance, the mustering point for disaffection since time immemorial. Generations of inbred ignorance perpetuated through inbred ignorance. They eyed her up as she glided past, furtively scratching their balls in the pockets of their oily jeans. She had been troubled a fleeting dissonance; the threatening intimidation of their unsolicited interest wrestling with a certain conceit that a woman in her forties can still stir teenage hormones.

Undaunted, she wandered into the tired-looking Co-op in search of nothing in particular. Well, perhaps a bottle or two of something to help medicate the demolition of her mother's existence and the need to numb the unravelling, raw emotions. The understocked grocery shelves housed the bare basics. The only isle burgeoned with products was where the crispy snacks met with alcohol. She had never realised that so many different brands of strong cider existed.

She might as well have been on another planet, so jarring was the town against the culture and sensibilities synonymous with her treasured city existence. There was no escaping that life is brutal, backward and uncompromising here. No prisoners taken and no mercy expected.

She had wandered back up to the house, head bowed and deep in thought. Apart from two bottles of Californian Merlot clinking in the polythene bag, it had been a fruitless and depressing crusade. She had already passed a couple of vaguely familiar faces touched by age before reaching the pedestrian crossing where she met the stooping figure of Mr Pritchard, the old postman. He paused and looked at her blankly, his face flushed by whisky and his breath shortened by fags. As a child he had surreptitiously slipped her Polo mints with a tweak of her cheek when she had met him at their gate. He would always comment on how much she had grown since he last saw her. Today, he stared through her, no light of recognition in his dulled, bleary eyes. She is anonymous. Forgotten.

The dog's interest in the smells of the bracken has petered out and he appears at her side nuzzling his wet nose against her elbow. She strokes his velvety jowls absent-mindedly. A clarity of thought has emerged that was previously elusive. Within a week the charity shops on the High Street will be filled with her mother's pointless trinkets. The house will be an empty shell, alien and unrecognisable, making her leaving easier. Her penultimate act prior to departure will be dropping the keys off at the estate agents.

On her way out of town, she will visit the cemetery where their ashes now both reside. A damp and gloomy hillside overlooking the A-road inland to the east and the only realistic option as their final resting place. She isn't one for graveside vigils nor lengthy heart-to-hearts with the departed. An attempt will be made to scrape moss from the marble and fresh flowers will be placed on the grave, not the putrid plastic imitations so favoured by the locals. A pot plant will last better maybe, for she won't be back for a good long time.

She will inhale deeply the crisp, unadulterated air one last time and pause before getting into her car. She will blow a kiss to her parents and thank them with devout sincerity once again for allowing her to escape. She will turn left out of the carpark and head east back to her normal life. Without regrets.

Old Age and Poverty

Some weekends, if their mood takes them, and their cars don't call for attention nor their lawns need mowing, the boys get off their fat arses and drive the twenty-minute round-trip to check whether The Old Fucker is still breathing. Occasionally, when feeling particularly benevolent, they bring him sweets in wrappers that he can't undo, fruit, just to annoy him, and his favourite, a Co-Op brand Neapolitan cake, which is deposited in the bread bin to grow mould. He nods a grudging thank you, staring blankly into the middle distance, maintaining an expression of withering disinterest.

Burdened by a growing apathy, they no longer bother to ask how he's faring, and these days dedicate only a few cursory, and wasted, minutes to their favourite subject of telling him what he should do, in full knowledge that he'll totally ignore all their well-intentioned advice. Their bland, middle-aged faces are barely able to disguise their disdain for this shell-of-a-man and his miserable predicament anymore. Like the cake, he is dry and pointless, long past his expiry date. They have lives to get on with, kids to endure, and mortgages to suffer. It is the source of much silent frustration that neither has yet managed to negotiate their way into holding the reins of his bank account. He may be daft, but he's not that far gone yet.

They hang around his cluttered home for half an hour or so, small talking in their usual awkward manner, eyeing up his tittle tattle and attaching their names to this and that, in preparation for when he's gone. They drink his tea, eat whatever that can find in his kitchen that's still in-date, and talk down to his frail form propped up askew in the metallic bulk of a hospital bed. They check their watches and leave casually, sharing a careless disregard that this could be the last time they see him alive. They're busy men with more pressing matters to address. Derek is a bigwig in the Scouts, and Luke has a wife, whose name the Old Fucker can no longer remember, with *problems.*

It's the hefty weight of history that tethers them all down in this pointless cul-de-sac. His embarrassment, and the inconvenience of God blessing him with two odd sons, as it was termed in the old days, late in life, when his career had been flying high. He had better things to do than kick a ball in the garden. Even now, older than he was then, they have never released the scalding grudge of being unceremoniously packed off out of sight and mind, to some second-rate South Coast boarding school where they were bullied relentlessly for the next seven years. Much of their lives have been overshadowed by a deep, repressed hatred, tempered by not wishing to upset their dominating mother. But no one expected that she'd shuffle off before him and following her untimely demise four years ago, it was time for the gloves to come off and put the Old Fucker clear on a few things.

Derek had decided to save petrol and put his thoughts in writing. A lengthy diatribe of vitriol and accusation, the phrasing straight out of his counsellor's textbook. His Mental Health Issues were solely placed at the feet of his father. His every failing sourced to the same malevolent, uncaring, negligent origin. It spilled out like vomit across the six pages of barely decipherable scrawl, leaving everyone confused and with a numb feeling of empty shitness. It hadn't been the cathartic epiphany that he had been anticipating and the Old

Fucker simply shook his bald, yellowing head, but remained tight-lipped as he sucked agitatedly on some butterscotch.

Luke's approach, aided and abetted by his unhinged betrothed, had been more direct. A tetchy and chaotic phone conversation with the Old Fuckers's GP had ruffled feathers and resulted in a Safeguarding referral. A number of awkward questions floated to the surface before it all fizzled into nothing as bureaucracy drowned in its own importance and higher priorities accumulated on all sides.

He should be in a home. Everyone knows that. But the time for relocation has long passed and this miserable existence is now his self-selected lot. Pride comes before a shit-show, monumental car crash and he's never been short of a measure of stubbornness. He wrote the fucking handbook.

Left for hours in solitude, The Old Fucker draws comfort from his meandering dialogues with Elsie. Her picture stares down at him from the wall wearing a characteristically forceful expression. She was never short of a point of view. These days, he occasionally wins an argument.

During his rare moments of wakefulness, when not conversing with Elsie, the Old Fucker ruminates constantly using the diminishing functional grey matter he has left to ruminate. Imagined arguments that merry-go-round in his head. Details that need ironing out. Things that need to be said before it's too late. The very many people who need to be put right. The boys, well, where do you start? Silly buggers, the pair of them. They both need a good cuffing around their ears. Elsie would have kept them in line and put paid to all their wet whining. If you can't say something good about someone, best shut up; that's how he was brought up. So, there's nothing left to be said.

And there are a few choice things he'd like to share with his carers, not a single one of them that should even be contemplated, let alone articulated in these enlightened times. Call a spade a spade, another staple of his youth. He mutters and groans as he lies in the dark, grimy, solitude of his own home, unsure if he's waiting for his carers or the grim reaper himself, and equally unsure whether he'll be able to tell the difference.

They do their best to sustain him with milky drinks which go untouched for the want of sufficient functionality to tip a cup. Small bowls of chocolate biscuits are left for him to snack on without consideration that he can't manage the wrapping paper. The Telegraph is pristine on a tray by his side, its recipient lacking the necessary dexterity to open its pages. He wistfully eyes the whisky bottle on the sideboard, wishing he could reach the bastard thing and self-medicate sufficiently to relieve all this suffering.

In lucid moments, he wishes that someone would have the gumption to clear the biscuit crumbs from under his chin but when they come, he is usually in a muddled daze, repeating the usual platitudes, and forgets to ask. And that fetid odour; someone should sort it out. He ponders the time when he was king. Sharp-suited with a conservative tie, he was something of a force to be reckoned with. He would bark out orders and people would listen. And act if they knew what was good for them. He hadn't acquired a company Jag for nothing. Hard graft and a good nose for business. He had a pension to match, now rapidly dwindling as the cost of paying someone to wipe his arse rises faster than inflation. These days his grey matter is too feeble to even recall his last meal.

He no longer has interest in the Monday horse-racing and his widescreen TV insolently stares back at him with a reciprocal blank expression. There is a moisture in his pyjamas that has uncertain origins. Although there remain doubts about the efficacy of the catheter, it is rare for him to be able to negotiate fluids into his mouth without some measure of spillage.

He listens to the incessant buzzing of the chainsaw next door. It is a trial of patience even with his challenged hearing and wizened brain. It would be enough to drive him to distraction if he had anything to be distracted from. The owner, a sour man with a rare and forgettable smile, who bears the burdens of the world heavily on his insipid, round shoulders, never calls around. He is too busy with his own life, penny pinching and grim-faced, waiting on his pension. He only communicates with people of use to him and the Old Fucker doesn't score any points in that category. There would be a mutual animosity if his neighbour gave a damn, and he could still muster enough fire in his belly.

The well-meaning couple from the other side pop around to jolly him along when their conscience pricks them sufficiently, and a spare five minutes can be found in their middle-class freneticism. They hold his hand and occasionally assist with the milky drinks while he repeats his questions about their health and kids. They ask If there's anything they can bring him and are met with the ubiquitous response of gold bars, delivered with the usual raspy chuckle. He hasn't lost his sense of humour they say, and there are few that doubt he will have the last laugh.

One day they'll find him on his rubber mattress, glassy-eyed and lifeless, moist pyjamas and yesterday's Telegraph untouched. They will find a Will in the dusty bureau that leaves everything to the boys. It's his final act of old-school decency and Elsie would not have sanctioned it any other way.

And yet, for now, he hangs on. An impish spark of torment still smoulders. The enzymes that lubricate his inner workings aren't exhausted yet. His kidneys churn out just enough to keep him above water and his lungs intake just sufficient to keep him afloat. And his irrepressible heart just keeps on beating, like it has something to prove, a big fat finger in the air to all his other failing organs. And one each for the boys.

Fucking Larkin Poe

From my vantage point at the back, I watch the sea of balding heads nodding gamely in rough synchrony with the relentless four/four rhythm booming from the stage. An army of bulbous prostates bobbing stoically up and down, most willing the song to finish so they can toddle off unobtrusively and join the toilet queue.

Some of the replete bladders have queued outside in cold, tight-lipped forbearance for hours, even though it's a standing-only venue and a non-sell-out gig. The majority are grandfathers, but they retain a rabid, competitive hunger to nab the best spot on the balcony and take blurry images on fiddly phones that they can't see in the dimmed lighting and fumble to use, never to be looked at again. They don't get out much these days.

Apart from on stage, there isn't a soul here under forty. Tonight, there is no delicate sweetness of weed hanging on the air; the only smell that wafts through the oppressive atmosphere is the stench of stale farts, fermented to the verge of putrefaction in aged bowels. The smattering of post-menopausal women who have been dragged along by enthusiastic partners look on in a bored, heavily made-up, collective glaze. Most are thankful that they're too short to be able to see the younger, more sexually charged sisters, strutting their stuff around the stage.

The maturity of the audience affirms new levels of appreciation for these ethereal visitors to our shores. A generation brought up on crackling vinyl, pompous over-complex concept albums and unnecessarily lengthy guitar solos is particularly receptive to this cacophonous, ballsy rock music, shunning the superficial light-weight

189

bollocks pumping out of Radio Two. This lot know their Strats from their Teles, and they know a searing riff when they hear one. They wear their threadbare Guns'n'Roses tee shirt with a certain pot-bellied pride.

I am stuck behind a man with an unfeasibly large head and can only catch glimpses of the attractive female singer fronting the show. She has a body like a gazelle and a voice ripped from Muddy Waters himself, demonstrating an enviable and effortless mastery over her maple fretboard. It isn't a stretch to explain the audience's skewed demographics.

She rocks and sways and postures. Mr Big Head in front keeps feeling the need to turn to his mate standing beside him, blocking my view even further, and expressing how fucking good she is. There is a palpable intake of breath from all around me when her tight white jeans bend over provocatively to the audience's great advantage, as she bids the drummer to end another song in unbridled crescendo.

I catch a glimpse of Jeff's perspiring brow as he turns to check his position in relation to the beckoning bar. Snarled up a row or two below and in front of where I've landed and I wonder how his atrial fibrillation is bearing up, still wearing his Anorak, in this rising heat. If he keels over, I can watch but would be powerless to help. I regret him telling me about his heart condition on the drive over, silence would have made for a better evening. I pray for his delicate constitution that his view of the guitarist's arse is obscured.

To collective relief, the band pause briefly and assemble around a single microphone centre stage with acoustic instruments. The whine of tinnitus in the room is of epidemic proportions. For some reason, they feel the need to wind up an otherwise excellent set with an Elton John cover. The audience is immediately divided. The hardened blues enthusiasts drop their arthritic shoulders in deflated shock, but the reluctant ladies suddenly seem to awaken, happy to trill along to the familiar chorus of Crocodile Rock.

There is a perceptible shake of the expansive cranium in front of me. I share his pain. I dip out towards the bar in the hope that Jeff is on the same wavelength and still has the strength in his legs to meet me there for the necessary tried and tested mode of revival.

Maud and Gilbert

Maud stares blankly at Gilbert through the cloud-grey half-light. Her gnarled fingers contort involuntarily into a pallid fist, engulfing her tired, non-descript wedding ring.

She could, if she had a mind.

Very deliberately, she puts the scissors down onto the teak sideboard festooned with his police memorabilia. This measly single-bedroom flat is all about his clutter and her meticulous dusting. Truncheons, medals and handcuffs jostle for attention between sepia eight by six framed huddles of grinning police cadets in stiff collars. Anyone would think the fucker had been with the rozzers the whole of his life.

His is a curious fascination given that Gilbert's history had, in fact, been somewhat less glorious. As a puller of pints in one of Manchester's less salubrious pubs and the quartermaster for a number of other shadier items unavailable from high street shops, he had camped for most of his life on the other side of the legal fence. Criminal was perhaps too strong a word for it, but his name had found its way into police enquiries on more than one occasion.

He had always possessed a certain panache, a rarity in his chosen trade and way off beam from his roots as the estranged son of a miner whose blackened hands matched his moods. Gilbert's eccentric dress sense and dry humour served as decoys for a multitude of sins. A man with outrageous front and pitiful depth, most of his life had been spent bluffing and cajoling his way out of sticky corners. And now look at his latest, grotesque incarnation, ponced up like a decrepit imitation of bloody Noel Coward in a pleated silk dressing gown and a plaid cravat. There's no one else within these four walls impressed by appearances. Not anymore. A dandy with a hairpin temper and a sharp right hand. She would still feel the latter if he could get his crippled arse out of that chair, although his physical infirmity doesn't prevent his vitriolic tongue from licking away at the festering wounds.

More pricks in you than a dartboard. A favourite staple of his. He would say it with a snaky grin on his face, both of them knowing the sprinkling of truth hidden within the rancorous words. For Maud's younger self had indeed led a colourful and expansive social life, mooching around with a certain enlightened crowd and availing herself fully to the advances in contraception the Sixties had offered. The frailties of the first wrinkle and an inch or two on the waist had led her to recognise the limitations of abandoned hedonism. And then came the night of their first meeting, she in an inebriated and disinhibited delirium, he pawing around her like a mongrel licking spilt milk. Truth be told, she had pondered many times over why she happened to end up with this particular prick.

I should have gone, many times over.

The wistful conversations she has with herself, sitting on the toilet, shaking her head, dabbing her eyes.

All those years ago, when Carol was small, I did it. I Did It. I left the bastard, steaming and raging, throwing threats and insults like they were hand grenades. I stuck it out in that damp bedsit with a squalling two-year-old for two weeks. Trying to dry nappies with a hairdryer. Going to bed at six in the evening because there was nothing else to do. Maybe that was it, the reason I came back. He showed the decency to wait until Carol was asleep before I got a black eye as a down-payment, and I've certainly paid a hefty levy of interest every day since.

He has been fighting a rear guard against the anger with her ever since. His every utterance is like an arm twist. His mean, miserly ways, the off-the-cuff spitefulness for its own sake and the distorted sense of indignant entitlement.

But now, scuppered by arthritis and a certain affliction of the brain, he spends his twilight days in the hazy hinterland between harumphing or snoring. Occasionally he calls on her to supply a sandwich or a blanket. She cannot remember a time when he had enquired about how her boat was floating. Most of his direct communication with her consisted of reminding her what a whore she had been and how her existence had been completely worthless until his benevolence had found her.

She stares out of the grimy kitchen window down at the muddy patch of scrubland beyond where a pair of kids are kicking a ball and pushing each other over. There is a dreadful tugging in her chest that reminds her that her own grandchildren no longer visit. She turns to look at the culprit, sitting on his own in the living room, staring into space. She eyes the knife rack. The fantasies of coming up behind him and putting the carving knife to his throat invade her consciousness on a daily basis. Truth-be-told, it would be a kindness to both of them if only she could find the courage. It must be stashed somewhere with all the other clutter in this pokey hellhole.

He calls her to bring his piss bottle. His aim isn't

great, and she knows it's deliberate. He presents it to her after completion like a prize, an earthy waft permeating from his slippers. *Thanks love,* he says, apparently oblivious to the unrelenting diatribe that has gone before. He's a fully certified one alright. One day she'll just throw it back over him.

There is a non-specific odour of rot around him. Of microbes invading and multiplying in places they shouldn't be. She has become used to it and only notices it when she comes in from shopping, huffing and puffing after hefting her wheely bag up the stairs. A first floor flat, what were they thinking when they moved here ten years ago?

The monotony is relieved by the doorbell's chime. She struggles down the stairs to open the door to the GP who beams unconvincingly before concocting an excuse to check on Gilbert's wellbeing. In truth the ambulance service has badgered him into a begrudged visit after repeated callouts to pick up the old boy off the floor.

It doesn't take long for the GP to realise the futility of his quest. Gilbert blethers on for twenty minutes, waxing lyrical about how good life is, and how they want for nothing, and how he keeps himself in shape doing exercises and stomping up and down the stairs each day. The GP nods attentively, stifles a yawn, and is cautious not to challenge. She is silent, nervous of his mouth later if she were to call him out and challenge this ridiculous depiction of geriatric Utopia. And she hates him even more for his pumped up lies and deception; she doesn't need reminding about just how perfectly trapped she is.

There are hushed words in the stairwell afterwards. The GP is sympathetic and can see the difficulties of her situation but ultimately offers nothing other than a helpline number for the domestically abused. Like she's going to share a room in some dingy hostel with a druggie twenty-year-old and her brats. She throws away the card into the old artillery shell casing that holds his various swords on her way back to the living room.

He looks at her smugly, pumped up with himself at selling the GP a dummy. "Silly fucker," he offers.

"I'm going out."

"What about my tea?"

"With all the exercise you're doing, you can make your own bloody tea for a change"

"You worthless tramp…"

But she is gone, scurrying down the stairs, anorak clenched in her hand.

"Don't forget your broomstick…"

The cold hits her. She has forgotten that it's December. The days melt into weeks and months in their dismal abode. Now she is outside without her purse or her bag or even her phone. She won't give him the satisfaction. She starts walking. She still has a good stride for her age, and she heads out of the retirement complex towards the town centre with a certain sense of purpose.

The Christmas lights illuminate the crepuscular drabness of the high street but fail to lift her. She passes a couple of drunk men in Santa hats singing Sweet Caroline, head down, hands deep in the pockets of her coat. There is a conker and a boiled sweet in her left, the flat keys and a piece of scrunched up paper in her right. She pulls it out and feels the flicker of excitement at unexpectedly discovering the ten-pound note.

With a renewed vigour she heads towards the hubbub of Wetherspoons, already bustling in the euphoria of after-work drinks. There is an unmistakable festive frisson inside. A twenty-two-year-old Maud would not have confidently approached the bar and ordered herself a large sweet sherry, and she certainly wouldn't have struck up a conversation with Tim and Eddie who happened to be sharing a pint or two in their work overalls. But there were many things that her younger self should and shouldn't have done and she doesn't have to think too long and hard to come up with a couple. The first sweet sherry squarely hits the spot, and the second softens it nicely.

It's another sweater colder under a black sky when she emerges with the first smile on her face that she can remember in a while. Tim and Eddie have made her laugh and kept her glass topped up with a gallant fervour. She had them in stitches when she told them snippets of Gilbert's idiocy over the years. It was like a confessional sponsored by Harveys Bristol Cream. A rediscovery of herself. She carries the glow of epiphany rather than any sense of guilt.

The pavement is slippery after a light rain and the car headlights glisten off the damp ground disorientating her. She totters a little. Her gait is a little less certain going back up the street than it had been coming down. It's been such a long time since...

***

She regains consciousness in an apparent warzone. Bright, clinical lights, a background hubbub that's both calm and frenetic at the same time. People attired in green and plastic aprons bustling around in all different directions. The noise level isn't conducive to a healing environment and is positively alarming for a muddled eighty-three-year-old with shattered bones lying in a puddle of her own piss.

In the old days, hospitals smelled of carbolic and efficiency. Now she reacclimatizes to the smell of vomit and alcohol and a certain corridor coldness to the air. A man with a bleeding head lurches around pointing his finger, shouting. A senior-looking nurse approaches him cautiously, and in soft tones, while her junior colleague hurries off to find security. Voices joust, accusatory and placatory.

Suddenly there is someone masked and inquisitive, shining lights at her eyes.

"Can you tell us your name, my love?"

Her tongue snags on jagged broken teeth. She croaks a response that even she can't understand. Notes are taken, the time is checked. She can hear a tutting from behind the mask and a subtle shaking of the head.

"You're in A&E, my love. I'm afraid you've had a bit of an accident," the voice is kindly but only a whisker away from being condescending. "Looks like you've hurt your hip."

The junior doctor still has spots. Maud considers asking her if she's started her periods yet but thinks it might be a tad disrespectful as she feels the searing pain of another hip examination. Something is administered through the tube in her arm and the warm levity of narcosis spreads through her broken body.

***

The man wearing a crumpled polythene apron incongruously over a tailored pinstripe suit lets out a long but barely perceptible sigh. A consummate professional, this is as far as he will go in demonstrating the intense frustration and irritation secreted inside his shiny, bald dome. Another private list cancelled because of this damn virus again; it's tantamount to bank robbery, and now being asked to cover the dismal post-take ward round because bloody Devlin has developed snuffles.

He scowls at the motley, round-shouldered crew that has assembled to accompany him on his whistle-stop tour around the new intake, like a posse rounding up stragglers. He dispenses with the niceties; let's get it over and done with then.

Effortlessly oozing pomposity, he strides over to Maud's bed in his most impressive consultoid manner, making the conscious gesture to soften his face when addressing her. He could win an Oscar for his approximation of empathy and sincerity.

"Good morning, Mrs McAvoy. It looks like you had a bit of a night of it..."

He is disconcerted to observe Maud beaming up at him and has to reconsult the x-ray images on the portable tablet he carries in case he might have missed something. Hers is some way removed from the usual patient demeanour on these early morning surveys of the wounded.

He cuts to the chase, judging that Mrs McAvoy appears to be short of a few marbles and not worthy of too much of his precious time.

"Looks like you had quite a nasty fall..., m'dear"

One of the nurses accompanying visibly cringes at his manner. Another giggles quietly behind her mask. Not much ever changes around here.

Unperturbed, he continues, pointing at the tablet for dramatic effect, "You've fractured your left hip rather badly... it must hurt?"

Maud nods but remains smiling demonstrating a full set of her own, slightly yellowed and now chipped, teeth.

Mr Bradley is bemused and blurts out a patronising chuckle.

"Maud, look I'm not sure you understand. You're going to have to have an operation, no small undertaking for someone of your vintage. And even then, your mobility is likely to be severely compromised." He peers at her notes again before delivering what he perceives will be the coup de grâce, "I can't see you ever being able to manage the stairs up to your flat again".

Maud closes her eyes briefly to fully absorb the joy of the moment. The man in the apron/pinstripe combo, who now has a noticeable flushing around the collar, is discombobulated and turns once again to the tablet, tapping it irritably and muttering inaudibly. But the rest of his crew observe a visible relaxation in the lines of her face, sixty years of hurt evaporating before their eyes. She puts her hands together in a gesture of prayer, raises her gaze to the heavens and mouths a prayer of thanks to the Deities responsible for broken and unhappy wives.

Ralph

Last night, his sofa snooze had been disturbed by his wife screaming at him to go and fuck himself and throwing her wedding ring at his dishevelled head. As he fumbled and failed to find a coherent response, she zipped off in the car, heading for her parents' place in leafy Surrey. Another weekend spent in the solitude of their grim single-bed flat in Wandsworth, as he sluggishly nudges his way up the surgical career ladder, had apparently been a step too far for her. That, and him being a total dick.

Prematurely returning from their honeymoon to allow him to attend an important lecture at the Royal College should perhaps have provided an enlightening enough insight into her horrible error, but like many before, she opted to endure several months of marital tolerance in the delusion that he might somehow reform into something resembling a normal human being.

The trials of marrying a disciple of the noble profession of surgery, her father had somewhat crassly put it, in between pompous puffs of his pipe and the self-absorption of his crossword. And now she's back under his self-opinionated feet, sleeping again under his self-satisfied roof.

One important skill that Ralph's chosen profession has bestowed on him is the normality of, and therefore the relative resilience to, sleepless nights. Witnessing the rise of the sun is very much part of the quotidian ritual of his chosen vocation, so in the combined absences of anyone to talk to over breakfast, and a car, he catches an early Tube, once again seeking solace in the familiarity of the grand edifice of one of the country's finest teaching hospitals.

The hour is early, and the entrance lobby is sparsely populated by people in a hurry. He treats himself to a date-expired egg sandwich from the unsanitary-looking vending machine while waiting for the lifts.

Away from the furore of the wards there exists a network of bleak anonymity. Corridors upon corridors of rooms inhabited by people doing something important who prefer to keep their doors closed. He slouches past a yawning cleaner reeking of BO, robotically pushing along a floor polisher, before turning another corner into the dimly lit purgatory, occupying the no man's land between the generator room below and the staff canteen above. Reaching a grubby, battle-worn door that bears the delusionally grandiose title of "Research Room", he fumbles for the keys, dropping the remains of his sandwich. Kicking open the door, he enters the small unwindowed box that contains nothing more than a coffee-stained desk, a creaky chair and a filing cabinet that doesn't close properly. But it's his, and that in itself is something of a feat given the enduring uncertainties overshadowing every other aspect of his life.

Feeling a confusion of depression and something approaching relief, he squeakily seats himself in an enforced slouch, turns on the laptop and concentrates hard on losing himself in the emotionally undemanding world of statistics and spreadsheets.

Minutes pass. The clanking of heating pipes and the buzz of the strip lights joust with his nasal breathing and the clicking of nimble fingers on the keyboard. The air hangs thick and static. He doesn't notice the scuttle of vermin doing their early morning rounds in the space above the polystyrene tiled ceiling. And he ignores the insistent bleeping from the pocket of his white coat hanging on the back of the door, as is his usual practice. It's one of the few skills he's managed to perfect in his eighteen months at this so-called centre of excellence.

He fiddles with his moustache subconsciously while trying to focus his mind on the glory of numbers. He knows, but prefers not to remind himself, that anyone with a modicum of self-respect would have already hung themselves by their Royal College tie from the hook on the back of the door that bears his white coat. But he's too tall for that, having to stoop to enter the room, and the hook is barely robust enough to hold said garment and its persistent, niggling contents. Spreadsheets triumph over suicide, at least this morning.

But they know where he is, and he can't hide for long in this grim prison of his own making. The days start inhumanely early on the surgical wards and the bedraggled housemen have been shuffling around awaiting his arrival on the ward for twenty minutes before deciding to go in search of him.

Shane appears first, looking like he's just tumbled out of a bed in the nurses' accommodation across the car park. He has at least managed to restore his wedding ring to its rightful place which isn't always the case. They stare at each other, baggy eyed and sleep-deprived for very different reasons. A heavy night on call, explains Shane.

Likeable but clueless, he's never short of a droll quip or two to camouflage his woeful ignorance. His quick wits and humour steer him precariously away from the brink of one life disaster to another. His flimsy grip of anatomy has been largely accumulated experientially rather than from the study of Gray's Anatomy. They give out medical degrees to any monkey who can write his name these days.

He lolls rakishly in the doorway with his white coat casually slung over his shoulder. He offers the sweetener of a lukewarm semblance of coffee from the machine by the lifts before launching a few ridiculously facile questions at his senior once again.

Ralph smiles paternally; there is no threat from this idiot. He just needs a bit of patient humouring, and he'll disappear back up to the ward to chat up student nurses again. A few sage words of guidance are issued, and off he scuttles like a man on a mission.

Ralph pushes the coffee to one side and enjoys a further few minutes of respite, immersed in the peaceful world of standard deviations from the mean before Rick appears. Unsmiling and like a dog with a bone, he's pissed off for having to waste his time finding the lazy bastard who won't answer his bleep. He too has spent a sleepless night looking at his clock, waiting for his pager to go off, even though he wasn't on call. Such is the primal effect of the malignant, little device.

He dispenses with the social niceties and demands decisions from the man who's paid to make them. He has a list of much the same queries as Shane, just framed in a more considered and probing way, and presented somewhat less affably. Clearly, they haven't conferred and as usual, Ralph dispatches him with terse, critical words and no tangible decisions.

Stung, and not for the first time, Rick retires, pulling faces which suggest a heady cocktail of anger, frustration and misery. In addition to the effects of insomnia, he carries a hefty hangover from the three hours he spent in the social club bar last night bemoaning his association with the occupant of the Research Room. He was fed some amusing information from a drunk theatre assistant, who had no right to know, of Jonathan's enthusiasm for intimate topiary as part of his foreplay, which he hadn't yet had the opportunity to share with Shane. The grating nuances of the C-word had been employed repeatedly and, along with a copious volume of Carlsberg, he had felt a whole lot better for a brief time.

A product of comprehensive education himself, Rick carries an innate hatred for this jumped-up, elitist institution and its pathetic products, like Ralph, who like obsequious lemmings, fall in line with the time-honoured traditions of brown-tongued servitude. He can't bear the thought of spending any longer than he has to in this nest of slithering, sycophantic, aspiring Masons. He fails to see how the living hell of life as a house officer can be construed in any meaningful way as a formative, learning experience. The best advice his senior ever offers is to go back and hit the books. It's unadulterated misery. They all need their fucking balloons popping. The sooner he can break out and join a GP training scheme, the better.

Rick's sole consolation for three months of torture is Ralph's aversion to spending time on the front line of the ward and his dislike for actually meeting the people he is about to dissect, so for the most part, he and Shane are largely left to their own devices. This is all well and good when the main activities are scribbling illegibly on drug charts and flirting with the new batch of student nurses, but less so when they find themselves out of their depth with a real clinical conundrum. It's lucky for them that Shane has charmed Paul, the brash Australian registrar on the neighbouring ward, who makes a point of smoking wherever he can get away with it in the hospital, into assuming the role of their rescuer, responding with hefty doses of Antipodean sarcasm to their panicked SOS's.

On the morning of a theatre list, it is customary for the senior registrar to circulate around the prospective victims with the house officers checking on the final surgical details and ensuring that everyone is as happy as they can be under the circumstances and consented. On rare occasions, when his glittering private practice allows, Mr Kennedy will also make an unenthusiastic although blustering appearance. Adorned in expensive suit and loud tie, the epitome of pomp and arrogance, a different Ralph will emerge into the role of attention-seeking schoolboy, cringing along in his wake, desperate to impress.

Today is a theatre day, and Shane and Rick have spent the last hour patching up their errors and concealing their oversights before Ralph eventually wanders onto the ward with a distinct lack of purpose. This, coupled with his somewhat unkempt appearance, suggests that Mr Kennedy is detained elsewhere. When he finds his housemen in their tiny alcove off the nurses' station, Shane is midway through a lurid explanation of what she did last night to make him spill his load.

Raised eyebrows indicate the need to get started on the ward round and they are joined by Steph, a staff nurse of head-turning looks and enviable efficiency. She nods a salutation to the assembly, lingers briefly in a complicit gaze with Shane and suggests they start with Harry Stein in the end bay.

The smell of bedpans mingles with breakfast and

disinfectant as they manoeuvre the obstinate notes trolley down the corridor. The cleaners bustle out their way like they're royalty, berating each other in Filipino. They are thankful of Steph's delicate trailing waft.

They pause at the end of the bed of a man who looks out of place, a good forty years younger and a few degrees sicker than the other patients. Shane surreptitiously extracts a pubic hair from his unbrushed teeth while Rick reads stiltedly from the twenty-six-year old's unhealthily thick, notes. He avoids the "occult malignancy" query, speaking so publicly. The ongoing bowel problems, the weight loss, the inconclusive scan result and now the need for last resort exploratory surgery.

Ralph smiles thinly and feigns his "relax, I'm in control" demeanour but miscalculates his phrasing badly, demonstrating an unimpressive cocktail of smugness, insincerity and condescension. He finishes by saying he'll do whatever it takes, and before further clarification can be sought, he's hand-sanitising and off to the next patient leaving the hapless housemen head scratching on the subject of consent.

The man looks alarmed and quizzical. Rick mouths to him that he'll be back in a minute before hastily catching up with the rest of the throng as they are treated to a crowd-pleasing view of the next patient's haemorrhoids.

They drag their way around the remaining three patients on the list, the only pleasant distraction from the trolley's incessant squeak is the sweet fragrance and endless possibilities that Steph leaves in her wake. They are lost in her redolent spell. Their powers of medical acumen dulled by a heady narcosis of female curves, so beautifully showcased by her darkly stockinged uniform.

"Right then, which of you is joining me upstairs?

Once again, Ralph spoils the moment.

The housemen are jolted back to reality by the unpleasant reminder that in the boss's absence, one of them will be required to accompany their ropey senior in theatre. Rick has a rising nausea from the previous night and could be more usefully employed than his unreliable counterpart on the ward duties, so naturally Ralph selects him as his lucky sidekick.

***

An hour later, the atmosphere in Theatre Four can be cut with a rusty knitting needle. McManus, the gasman unwillingly assigned to the list, hates Ralph with a barely concealed vehemence. Ralph hates McManus, realising that the wily Irishman can see through the old school tie façade and mindless bluster to the imposter underneath. Rick, the miserable junior heaving back the retractors prizing open the hole cut in Harry Stein's abdomen, hates everything about theatre. He battles the urge to vomit, an unfortunate and recurring predicament when hungover, scrubbed up under the bright theatre lights, facing the bloody gore.

Staff Nurse Miles says little but sees everything as she passes the instruments that Ralph demands with a quiet, measured efficiency. She hates all doctors, but she particularly despises the fact that she depends on them to pay off her mortgage. She has witnessed so many of these stupid clashes of inflated egos over the years, the little peacocks strutting and sparring, she could write the fucking book. She observes time and again, that something deeply unpleasant happens to most of them when the prefix DR is acquired before a name, and something worse again when it's traded back for the surgical holy grail of MR.

The young student nurse with the misfortune of having been assigned Theatre Four for the afternoon cowers in the corner, hoping to go unnoticed. This isn't at all the rose-tinted heroics she had imagined. She has scanned the room for an ally and found none. She feels a deep discomfort but isn't sure why. She would be biting her nails had she not been forced to wear sterile virtual strait jacket of mask and gloves.

Having anaesthetised the patient, McManus starts a crossword and, refusing to pull his mask over his bulbous, ruddy nose, exhales tobacco fumes down the bloody mess of the business end.

A mutual animosity smoulders across the green drape separating the head from the chaos of intestines with which Rick, wrestles unconvincingly. Ralph is tetchy and tutting, partly over the ineptitude of his assistant, but also with the findings inside.

"Right, we're done here."

McManus raises a quizzical bushy eyebrow but says nothing. Rick looks flummoxed. He hasn't really been concentrating, but he's pretty certain that Ralph hasn't done anything other than open up the abdomen and rummage around a bit in a sea of blood, fat and omentum.

"It's hopeless" Ralph says by way of explanation. "He's riddled with it. Christ knows why those clowns in radiology couldn't pick this up from the scan."

He pauses briefly before appealing for a witness.

"I mean, even YOU can see…?"

Rick cannot see but it seems simplest to just

acquiesce and nod.

"Right let's zip him up and finish this." He throws a glance over the green drape. "I think it's best that we make sure he doesn't wake up".

There is a barely perceptible shake of the head, but the frowning McManus will not be drawn away from 6 down.

The objection comes from the opposite side of the theatre table.

"What do you mean 'doesn't wake up?' You can't do that!"

"Why's that?"

"Because you're playing God... You have no right!"

Ralph is quiet for a couple of minutes as he wrestles with the deep sutures.

"Right, you finish off the skin" he hands Rick the forceps with hefty measure of passive aggression and turns to leave.

"I've spoken to his mother. We're doing him a favour." He pauses for effect. "You have a lot to learn."

The remainder of the list is spent in a tense silence apart from the gurgling of the suction and Ralph's muffled humming from behind his mask. He is pondering statistics and spreadsheets. McManus has chosen to observe a sullen silence rather than offer his views on Ralph's management plan. Staff Nurse Miles maintains her routine of wordless, ruthless efficiency but has made the decision that she needs to have a quiet word in Mr Kennedy's ear when he next deigns them with his presence.

Rick's nausea has turned to disgust, as his hungover brain struggles to process the ethical dilemma that has unexpectedly presented itself. There seems to be something very wrong afoot but as a medical peon he feels totally powerless. He realises too late that he forgot his promise to return to Harry Stein in the confusion of being summoned to theatres. It suddenly feels like an important missed conversation.

They all limp through to the evening.

After a couple of hours filling in forms and changing catheters, Rick cannot face trying to conjure up something to eat when he gets back to his flat, so he heads straight for the social club for the nourishment of cheese and onion crisps and lager. McManus is at the bar and insists on buying a round of half and halfs; Special Brew and Carlsberg. Does the job but with less pain in the morning, so he says. He avoids any mention of the afternoon in Theatre Four and, as a fairly transparent distraction tactic, recalls a far-fetched and much-embellished story about Ralph being caught shagging one of the theatre assistants behind a curtain in the recovery room.

There is a brief lift as Rick spots Steph's arrival, dressed up like she means business, only to feel the deflation of her cursory nod as she drifts past to meet Paul in the outside smoking area, even though she doesn't smoke.

Further rounds are downed, and Rick returns to his room in the doctor's accommodation, numbed and hoping that he's sufficiently anaesthetised to sleep tonight.

Shane's wife hasn't seen him for a couple of days and has put on her eye make-up and glossed her pouting lips. She has cooked him a special dinner and tells him that she's pregnant. They toast, and he falls asleep in a dribbling heap in front of the television.

Ralph throws his keys on the table, the noise echoing around his empty flat, and eyes up the transverse ceiling rafter in his vaulted kitchen. Turning off his phone, he removes his tie and contemplates it for a moment before pulling up a chair and standing on it.

Facebook Friends

I'm caught off guard and my fists are balls of white-knuckle clenched rage once again. It seems to be happening with increasing and uncomfortable frequency as my addiction grows.

Not so long ago, if I had felt the need for stimulation, a simple walk might have sufficed. Maybe a fiddle with the car, a poke around the dilapidated plants in the garden or even a game of golf if I felt adventurous. Nowadays I can get my kicks with just the simple acts of lifting of a laptop lid and sticking the kettle on.

My evil computer miraculously knows where to take me; the log ins are automatic, the time-wasting blue circle as good as absent. I head for the usual destination.

WTF!

Righteous indignation is the common thread in most of Spike's posts. Today his ire is directed at a failure of communication from the district council about changes to the recycling collection schedule. Without pausing, our noble ambassador for all that should be right in the world goes on to question the opening hours of Widdowson's DIY store and how the fuck you get an appointment at the local GP surgery. He adds, somewhat disingenuously, that most people working for the NHS are lazy arses and should pull their fingers out, finishing with a flurry of GIFs of someone with hands in the air, scowling yellow face, head on fire.

I don't need reminding that Spike's pathway through life is hardly a shining inspiration to us all. He is in his mid-fifties, jobless for reasons that aren't entirely clear, and living with his elderly mother in some obscure backwater in Shropshire. We shared a childhood friendship loosely based around playing football but mostly just kicking each other. I was bigger than him back then so generally gained the upper hand. Clearly that's where it should have all ended.

My sole contact with him these days is through this inauspicious medium and it's all strictly one-way. For no matter how much the pettiness of his commentary stirs my bile, I have made a conscious decision against responding in such a public arena. Shitting on my own doorstep is the phrase that comes to mind. I distinctly remember being warned against it as a wayward teenager by my parents. The trouble is, these days, it's impossible to spot where your doorstep starts and ends.

Today, Spike's whinings don't hold my attention for long, containing even more irrelevancies than usual and I am intrigued to see old Dicky has logged in again after a noticeable absence.

Dicky Mount, another wingman from our teens, has a penchant for punching out volleys of distasteful right-wing rhetoric. Christ knows what bunch of fascist loons are hooked into his followers. There's something about those with far-right leanings that seem to give them a deranged sense of entitlement that they can spout any shade of bollocks with authority. Loads of bullshit with Union Jacks, BREXIT and choice quotes from the collected wisdom of Nigel Farage. To think of the white, middle-class, heterosexual Utopia we could be living in now if only Enoch Powell had become Prime Minister way-back-when. It all makes me shudder, but still, I can't help myself being drawn in by these desperate missives.

He and Spike are Friends and frequently Like each other. Thumbs up, pal. Ha Ha! Throaty, laughy face. The meeting of small minds across a vast ether, each stoking on the other with ever more outrageous and ridiculous opinions. How could a force for such good be taken over by the simple-minded?

His targets of derision today are the upper echelons of the Labour Party; a soft prey granted, but he sounds like he's just spouting from a Daily Mail opinion column, his views lacking any depth, imagination or originality. He forgets the K and the W when he writes no and not enough O's on his to's either. His political opinion remains as nuanced as his spelling.

Not for the first time I consider subscribing his profile to a gay dating site. Laughing yellow face. Thumbs up. Pal. But I worry that my digital ineptitude will break my cover and expose me. Maybe one for another day, when I've finally figured out what I'm doing. Until then, I must consign myself to the voyeuristic side-lines.

Ever the antidote, Evan Bun, the overweight, docile kid from school who used to get pushed around a fair bit and now works in some bakery in Kidderminster, has clearly reinvented himself as a bit of a biker these days. He likes to post endless video clips of Motorcycle Grand Prix races which, to those not sharing the depth of his enthusiasm, just seem like a load of noise and speed on repeat.

He has contrived to grow his hair long and greasy and looks no less dreary than he ever did. He wears his leather jacket with a confident pride over a stout beer-belly and has concocted some authentic-looking grease stains on his jeans. None of his posts appear to contain him in the presence of a motorbike as such, just looking pissed up with a half-drunk bottle of Newcie Brown and a bunch of similarly dressed saddos, usually posing with middle fingers up to the camera. Not an abundance of women in them either, I notice. At least none that are recognisable as such. No matter what misfortunes I'm enduring, he always manages to make me feel better about myself does Evan.

Subconsciously, I find that I have entered the word TWAT in capital letters in the comments box. Delete and scroll down...

Continuing to irritate me, even via the infinite expanse of the Internet is Tricia, an acquaintance from distant student days, who has suddenly started posting regularly, like she's just discovered it. She has clearly married well and moves with a somewhat different set these days. Today she has posted an image of the damage done to her husband's Aston when he smashed into an unsuspecting pheasant, making some flippant quip about the birds exacting their revenge for the number he's taken down over the years. Blood sports enthusiast and show off; it just gets better and better. Laugh-head-off face.

My fingers twitch over a keyboard willing me into words I'll regret, enticing me to go public with my vexations and unleash both barrels. Most of all I want to tell her that no one gives a fuck about her or her la-di-dah lifestyle and offer some suggestions on better uses for her esteemed husband's gun. There are so many more potential comments that rush into my brain all at once and I am temporarily confused.

I take a deep breath, sip my cooling coffee and ponder on Tricia's intent. Blatant conceit versus tactless insensitivity. Neither were really her thing as I recall back in the old days. I consider her other recent posts relating to a daughter, who naturally looks like a fashion model, qualifying as a ski-instructor in Verbier, and a shot of an expansive, well-kept lawn leading down to a river where an expensive-looking yacht is moored. Some sort of quip about the frequency of mowing and needing a machete to go out for a sail. Bless. She does rather labour her point.

I conclude, not for the first time, that I don't like her but can't bring myself to click delete from my contact list. After all, this stuff is so much more entertaining than Netflix.

Adie, another B-league friend from thirty years ago, has posted some more old-school cartoons, mostly focused on alcohol. They're funny in a passing chuckle sense, but I can't help wondering whether his real motive is to validate some of the frailties in his own life. He posts images of pints in various pubs and bars. Last year, we were treated to a pint-by-pint guide to Lanzarote, most with sunsets in the background. One, apparently a sunrise. Maybe he should write the definitive guidebook if only he could find a hiatus of sobriety.

Happiness isn't about getting what you want all the time. It's about loving what you have and being grateful for it.

Cheryl signposts us to a yoga workshop in which we can all find our inner truth and heal ourselves. There is an image of a lithe, fit-looking woman in a leotard, who looks physically as far removed from Cheryl as its possible to be. She's constantly posting garbage about emancipating the strong woman inside of her. I resist the temptation to comment and suggest that I think there may be more than one in there. Always be kind, as she would commend, it is the manna that sustains us.

Life is clearly pretty good for Jerry who is once again

very pleased with himself at having retired early. Dull as the proverbial accountant that he was until the age of fifty-five, he seems to have embarked upon a phoenix-like rebirth now that he's drawing a substantial pension and driving around Cornwall in a soft-top Porsche. And doesn't he like to tell us about it?

Smugly installed in some swish retirement apartments near St Michaels's Mount, where it apparently never rains, every post shines brightly with pristine skies and the broad, self-congratulatory grins. Golf today, tennis tomorrow. Last week he was busy on some cookery course, learning the versatility of seaweed as a humble ingredient. And he's considerate enough to share images of every last moment with us. When on earth does he find the time to upload this drivel?

I continue my scroll down through adverts enticing me to buy stuff I don't need from Amazon, but the fun is waning. I begin to realise why I'm no longer in touch with these people and how we remain "friends" only within the sterile confines of social media. I have nothing in common with any of them other than a shared history at some point which was tenuous at best in the majority of cases. The names of my true friends don't even feature on my list of shared contacts.

Someone has clearly been looking over my shoulder on recent web-searches and I'm now receiving an almost daily barrage of golf porn. I save the website to revisit later, my Visa Card might yet take another beating.

Friend request.

A dreary ex-colleague wants to reinvigorate my contacts list to the tune of one and I again wrestle with a dilemma of etiquette. Truth is, I don't give a flying fuck what Fabian is up to these days but nor do I dislike him sufficiently to cause offence by declining his request. I decide that on balance there may be more entertainment gained through acceptance, and I am reminded of dear Cheryl's wisdom that one can only find one's true self by being open to others. WTF. Accept. Wave.

Give generously. Delete

And here's a detailed map and elevation chart informing me of how far Piers has cycled today with his long-suffering wife, Mandy, the emphasis firmly on marital bliss and shared experiences. He has led, obviously, and she has dutifully puffed along, staring at his Lycraed arse for two miserable hours. At least that's arguably his best feature. He doesn't boast quite so publicly when he's been caught out riding his secretary. The sheer vanity that anyone might care how many hills he's conquered today is astonishing. How many calories he burns in his office, "at work" would be so much more interesting.

Some fuckwit on the Village Collective stream has decided to post some images of dog turds on the grass verge outside the Community Centre with the comment, *Why?*

Because dogs have to go somewhere, and you need to find something more fulfilling in life than pointing your phone at dog poo. I have typed my response subconsciously but am restrained by my left brain before my twitchy finger presses post.

Take time to notice the small things in life.

WTF!

Spike has re-emerged into this narcissist's paradise, holding forth about some bloke in a passing brown Vauxhall who gave him the finger while he was standing outside the Londis lighting a cigarette. What is the world coming to?

Be the reason someone feels welcome, seen, heard, valued, loved and supported.

We are all but a single click away from deletion.

Acknowledgements

My thanks to Mr Taylor and Miss Williams, my first English teachers, for igniting my interest in writing fiction. It has been a slow train coming.

My short stories would never have seen the light of day without the support of the wonderful people at the Society of Medical Writers whose competitions sustained and uplifted me through the COVID pandemic. I am particularly grateful to Neil Wilson and Moira Brimacombe for their positive feedback and unerring encouragement.

I will always be happy to stand my good friend Martin Harman for a pint of ginger beer shandy in acknowledgement of his brilliant legal skills, emancipating my work from the clutches of evil publishing forces.

Similar gratitude to my fellow authors Phil Whittaker and Taliesin Nye, who both offered me invaluable wisdom, feedback and encouragement.

Follow your dreams Phoebe Jones, your artistic skills are a wonderful gift, and your ability to decipher my unworthy directions is truly remarkable.

I am forever indebted to Oliver Eade for his interest in my writing, his encouragement and his gentle and expert guidance. This book would not have existed without him.

I am honoured to be an author under Silver Quill Publishing and very grateful to Wendy Leighton-Porter for allowing me this opportunity.

Finally, thanks to my wonderful Fam (J, W, P and G) for their love, laughs and indulgence. How lucky am I? Couldn't have done it without you all.

AUTHOR PAGE

Christopher C James is a retired GP, having worked in the NHS for over thirty years. He was born in Wales and currently lives in the West Country of England.

Unredacted Expletives is his first published work of fiction.

Christopher C James is a pseudonym.

Facebook:
Christopher C James – Author

If you have enjoyed Unredacted Expletives, please post a review to help other readers find it.

ABOUT SILVER QUILL PUBLISHING

Silver Quill is an independent publishing group, producing fabulous books for children, teens, young - and not so young - adults. Take a look at our website, meet our authors and browse through the titles we have to offer. Every book is a thrill with Silver Quill!

www.silverquillpublishing.com

Printed in Great Britain
by Amazon